Dear Reader,

The Watcher in the Shadows is the third of the novels I wrote for younger readers at the beginning of my career in the 1990s. How young is young when it comes to reading is a tricky question and one I've never been able to answer. As with many things in life, it depends. When I wrote these books I was aiming to write the kind of novel I would have liked to read when I was 12 or 13 years old. I was trying to offer a nod to all the books kids of my generation used to read, from the mysteries of Enid Blyton to the great 19th-century classic stories of intrigue and adventure from Dumas to Verne to Stevenson and beyond. I was also secretly hoping that adult readers would enjoy them as well, and that the novels would hopefully transport them back to those first books that capture a reader's imagination and fire a love for literature. A world of heroes, villains, magic and adventure, a world in which children fight and love and live intensely and don't spend their entire dreamlives texting or surfing the net with virtual friends. These novels deliberately hark back to bygone days. They remind me of what the discovery of reading meant to me. I hope they remind you too, regardless of your age. So, how young is young? It depends. Mostly, on you!

Happy travels,

Carlos Ruiz Zafón

THE WATCHER IN THE SHADOWS

CARLOS RUIZ ZAFÓN

TRANSLATED BY
LUCIA GRAVES

To place orders in the U.S., please contact your Hachette Book Group sales representative or call Hachette Customer Service, toll-free: 1-800-759-0190.

This is an uncorrected proof. Please note that any quotes for reviews must be checked against the finished book. Dates, prices, and manufacturing details are subject to change or cancellation without notice.

LITTLE, BROWN AND COMPANY
New York · Boston

Little, Brown and Company

Hachette Book Group
237 Park Avenue, New York, NY 10017
Visit our website at www.lb-teens.com

Little, Brown and Company is a division of Hachette Book Group, Inc.
The Little, Brown name and logo are trademarks of Hachette Book Group, Inc.

The publisher is not responsible for websites (or their content) that are not
owned by the publisher.

First U.S. Edition: May 2012

[CIP to come; ISBN 978-0-316-04476-9]

10 9 8 7 6 5 4 3 2 1

RRD-C

Printed in the United States of America

THE
WATCHER
IN THE
SHADOWS

Dear Irene,

Sometimes I think I am doomed never to forget the mirage of that summer we spent together in Blue Bay. You'd be surprised to see how little things have changed since those days. The lighthouse still rises through the haze like a sentry, and the road that runs alongside the Englishman's Beach is now just a feint track snaking through the sand to nowhere.

The ruins of Cravenmoore peer through the forest, silent and shrouded in darkness. On the increasingly rare occasions when I venture into the bay on my sailing boat, I can still see the cracked windowpanes of the west wing. Sometimes I imagine I can see the lights again, flickering in the twilight. But I know that nobody lives there any more. Nobody.

You will probably wonder what has become of the house on the headland, Seaview. Well, it's still there, isolated, facing the vast ocean up on the clifftop. Last winter a storm carried away what was left of the small jetty on the beach below. A wealthy jeweller from some nameless town was tempted to buy the house for next to nothing, but the westerly winds and the pounding of the waves against the cliffs managed to dissuade him. The salty air has made its mark on the white wood, and the secret path that led to the lagoon has become an impenetrable jungle, overrun with wild bushes and strewn with fallen branches.

From time to time, whenever my work down at the dock allows it, I get on my bike and cycle up to the headland to watch the sunset from the porch: just me and a flock of seagulls that have moved in without even bothering to ask permission from the estate agent. From up there you can still see the moon casting its silver thread towards the Cave of Bats as it rises over the horizon.

I remember that I once spun you a story about this cave: a tale about a sinister pirate whose ship was devoured by the grotto one night in 1746. It was a lie. There never were any smugglers or buccaneers who sailed into the shadows of that cave. In my defence, this was the only lie you ever heard from my lips. Although you probably knew from the start.

This morning, as I was hauling in a tangle of nets that had snagged on the reef, it happened again. For a split second I thought I could see you, standing on the porch of Seaview gazing quietly out to sea, as you used to. But when the seagulls rose from the building and flew away I realised there was nobody there. Further up the coast, Mont-Saint-Michel hovered above the mist like a fugitive island that had run aground at low tide.

Sometimes I think that everyone has disappeared to some other place, far from Blue Bay, and only I have remained here, trapped in time, waiting in vain for the tide to bring back something other than memories.

I think this must be the hundredth letter I've sent to the last address I could find for you in Paris. Sometimes I wonder whether you've received any of my letters, and whether you still remember me and that dawn on the Englishman's Beach. Maybe you do; or maybe life has taken you far from here, far from the memories of the war.

Life was much simpler then, wasn't it? But what am I saying? Surely that's not true. I'm beginning to think that only I am foolish enough to go on reliving each and every one of those days in 1937, when you were still here, by my side . . .

1. THE SKY OVER PARIS

Paris, 1936

Those who remember the night Armand Sauvelle passed away would swear that a purple light flashed across the sky, leaving in its wake a trail of blazing ashes that faded away over the horizon; a light that his daughter Irene never saw but which would haunt her dreams for years to come.

It was a cold winter's dawn and the windowpanes in Ward 14 of Saint George's Hospital were covered in a film of ice.

Armand Sauvelle's flame went out silently, without so much as a sigh. His wife Simone and his daughter Irene looked up as the first glimmer of day cast needles of light across the hospital ward. His youngest child, Dorian, was asleep on one of the chairs. A heart-rending stillness filled the room. No words were necessary to explain what had happened. After six months of suffering, an illness whose name he was never able to pronounce had snatched away Armand Sauvelle's life.

It was the beginning of the worst year the Sauvelle

family would ever experience.

Armand Sauvelle took his charm and his infectious laughter with him to the grave, but his numerous debts did not accompany him on his final journey. Soon a whole horde of creditors and vultures wearing elegant frock coats began to drop by the Sauvelles' home in boulevard Haussmann. After the legal niceties of those first visits came the veiled threats. And these soon gave way to the seizure of the family's assets.

Prestigious schools and beautifully tailored clothes were replaced by part-time jobs and simpler outfits for Irene and Dorian. This was the beginning of the Sauvelles' spectacular fall into the real world. The one who came off the worst, however, was Simone. Returning to her job as a teacher did not provide enough income to stem the torrent of debt that consumed their limited resources. New documents signed by Armand seemed to crop up everywhere: a seemingly bottomless rabbit hole of unpaid loans and letters of credit.

By this point young Dorian had begun to suspect that half the population of Paris was made up of lawyers and accountants, a special breed of ravenous rodent that lived above ground. Also by then, and without telling her mother, Irene had taken a job in a dance hall. For just a few coins (which, in the early hours, she would slip into the box Simone kept hidden under the kitchen sink), she would dance with clumsy young soldiers with sweaty hands who were really no more than frightened children themselves.

At the same time, the Sauvelles discovered that the list of people who used to call themselves friends was evaporating like dew in the morning sun. That summer, however, Henri Laffont, an old friend of Armand Sauvelle, offered the family a small apartment above the art shop he managed in Montparnasse. He waved aside the rent – to be repaid in better times – all he asked in exchange was Dorian's assistance as an errand boy, because his knees were no longer what they had once been. Simone could never find enough words with which to thank old Monsieur Laffont for his kindness. But the shopkeeper didn't expect any thanks. In a world of rats they'd happened on an angel.

As the first days of winter sent a chill through the streets, Irene turned fourteen years of age, although they felt more like twenty-four. For once, she spent the coins she earned in the dance hall on herself and bought a cake with which to celebrate her birthday with Simone and Dorian. Armand's absence still weighed on them like an oppressive shadow. They blew out the candles together in the narrow sitting room of their apartment on the rue de Rennes, making a wish that the bad luck that had been hounding them for months would be extinguished along with the flames. For once, their wish was not ignored. Although they were still unaware of it, the year of darkness was coming to an end.

Some weeks later a ray of hope unexpectedly burst into

the lives of the Sauvelle family. Thanks to the influence of Monsieur Laffont and his network of acquaintances, Simone was offered a good job in Blue Bay, a small village on the coast far from the dreary greyness of Paris and from the sad memories of Armand Sauvelle's last days. Apparently, a wealthy inventor and toy manufacturer named Lazarus Jann needed a housekeeper to take care of his palatial residence amid the forest of Cravenmoore.

The inventor lived in a huge mansion next to his old toy factory, which was now closed, with his wife Alexandra, who was seriously ill and had been bedridden for twenty years. The pay was generous and besides, Lazarus Jann was offering them the possibility of moving into Seaview, a modest house that stood on the edge of the cliffs on the other side of Cravenmoore forest.

In the middle of June 1937 Monsieur Laffont bid goodbye to the Sauvelle family on Platform 6 of the Gare du Nord. Simone and her two children boarded the train that was to take them to the Normandy coast. As Monsieur Laffont watched the carriages disappear into the distance, he smiled to himself for a moment – he had the feeling that the story of the Sauvelles, their real story, had only just begun.

2. GEOGRAPHY AND ANATOMY

Normandy, summer of 1937

On their first day at Seaview, Irene and her mother tried to instil some sort of order into what was to be their new home. Meanwhile Dorian discovered a new passion: geography or, to be precise, map making. Equipped with the pencils and drawing book Henri Laffont had given him as a parting gift, Simone Sauvelle's younger child retreated to a spot on the cliffs, a vantage point from which he could enjoy the spectacular view.

The village with its small fishing dock occupied the centre of the large bay. To the east, an endless expanse of white sand, known as the Englishman's Beach, stretched along the water's edge. Further on, the narrow point of the headland jutted out into the sea like a giant claw, separating Blue Bay from the wide gulf the locals called Black Bay, because of its dark, deep waters. The Sauvelles' new home was perched on the very tip of the headland.

Half a mile out to sea, Dorian detected a small island with a lighthouse. The lighthouse tower stood dark and mysterious, its edges blurred by the shimmering haze. Turning his head back towards land, he could see his sister Irene and his mother standing on the porch of the house.

Seaview was a two-storey building of white timber perched on the clifftop. Behind it grew a thick forest and, just above the treetops, he could see the majestic residence of Lazarus Jann: Cravenmoore.

Cravenmoore looked more like a castle than a home, the product of an extravagant and twisted imagination. A cathedral-like construction of arches, flying buttresses, towers and domes adorned its angular roof. The building itself was shaped like a cross, with various wings sprouting from it. An army of gargoyles and stone angels guarded the façade like a flock of petrified spectres. As Dorian closed his drawing book and prepared to return to Seaview, he wondered what kind of person would choose to live in a place like that. He would soon find out: that night they had been invited to dine at Cravenmoore, courtesy of their new benefactor.

Irene's new bedroom faced north-west. Gazing out of her window she could see the lighthouse and the patches of light cast by the sun over the ocean. After months of being imprisoned in the tiny Paris flat, the luxury of having a room to herself and being able to close the door and enjoy her own private space felt sinfully good.

As she watched the sea turn to copper in the setting

sun, Irene faced the dilemma of what to wear for her first dinner with Lazarus Jann. She had only a few items left from what had once been a huge wardrobe, and the idea of being received at Cravenmoore mansion made all her dresses seem like embarrassing old rags. After trying on the only two outfits that might do, Irene noticed another problem she hadn't counted on.

Ever since she had turned thirteen, her body had insisted on adding volume in some places and losing it in others. Now, close to her fifteenth birthday, Irene was more aware than ever of the influence of nature as she looked in the mirror. The severe cut of her drab clothes did not match her new curvaceous shape.

Shortly before nightfall, Simone Sauvelle rapped gently on Irene's door.

'Come in.'

Her mother closed the door behind her and quickly scanned the situation. All of Irene's dresses were laid out on the bed. Wearing only a plain white vest, her daughter was kneeling by the window, staring out at the distant lights of the ships in the Channel. Simone observed Irene's slender body and smiled to herself.

'Time flies and we don't even notice, do we?'

'None of them fits me. I'm sorry,' Irene replied. 'I've tried.'

Simone went over to the window and knelt down next to her daughter. In the middle of the bay the lights of the village spread ripples of colour over the water. For a moment, they both gazed at the spectacle. Simone stroked her daughter's face and smiled.

'I think we're going to like this place. What do you think?' she asked.

'But what about us? Is he going to like *us*?'

'Mr Jann?'

Irene nodded.

'We're a charming family. He'll love us,' replied Simone.

'Are you sure?'

'I certainly hope so.'

Irene pointed to her clothes.

'Wear something of mine.' Simone smiled. 'I think my dresses will look better on you than they do on me.'

Irene blushed. 'Don't exaggerate.'

'Just you wait and see.'

Dorian's expression was priceless when he saw his sister arrive at the foot of the stairs draped in one of Simone's dresses. Irene fixed her green eyes on her brother and raised a threatening finger.

'Not one word,' she warned.

Dorian nodded mutely, unable to take his eyes off this stranger who spoke with the same voice as his sister Irene. Simone noticed this and tried not to smile. She placed a hand on the boy's shoulder and knelt down to straighten the purple bow tie he had inherited from his father.

'You'll spend your life surrounded by women, son. You'd better start getting used to it.'

By the time the clock on the wall struck eight they were all ready for the great event, dressed in their smartest clothes. They were also terrified.

A light breeze blowing in from the sea stirred the thick forest surrounding Cravenmoore. The rustling of invisible leaves accompanied their footsteps as Simone and her two children walked along the path through the wood. A pale moon struggled to break through the canopy of shadows and hidden birds nesting in the crowns of the century-old giants called out to each other in an unnerving chorus.

'This place gives me the creeps,' said Irene.

'Nonsense,' her mother snapped. 'It's only a wood. On you go.'

From his position at the rear Dorian glanced around at the twisted forms of the vegetation. In the darkness his imagination transformed the sinister shapes into dozens of evil creatures lying in wait.

'In the daylight you'll see there's nothing out there but bushes and trees,' said Simone Sauvelle, not sounding entirely sure herself.

A few minutes later, after a trek that Irene thought was never going to end, the imposing profile of Cravenmoore stood before them. Golden beams of light shone from the large windows beneath a jagged forest of gargoyles. Beyond the house they could make out the toy factory, an annex to the main building.

Once they were out of the forest, Simone and her children stopped to contemplate the immensity of the toymaker's residence. Suddenly a bird that looked like a crow emerged from the undergrowth, flapped its wings and took off, taking a curious route over the gardens that surrounded Cravenmoore. After circling one of the stone fountains it alighted at Dorian's feet. After it had stopped flapping its wings, the crow lay on its side and began to rocked gently to and fro until it came to rest. Dorian knelt down and cautiously stretched out his right hand.

'Be careful,' warned Irene.

Ignoring her advice, Dorian stroked the crow's feathers. The bird showed no signs of life. He lifted it up and unfolded its wings. Dorian looked puzzled, then dismayed. He turned to Irene and Simone.

'It's made of wood,' he murmured.

They all looked at one another. Simone sighed.

'Let's just make a good impression, all right?' she begged her children.

They both nodded in agreement. Dorian placed the bird back on the ground. Simone Sauvelle gave a hint of a smile and then all three climbed the white marble staircase that snaked towards the large bronze entrance.

The doors of Cravenmoore opened automatically, before they'd even had time to use the brass knocker, which was shaped like an angel's face. A figure stood in the doorway, silhouetted against the aura of light that poured from the house. The figure suddenly came alive, tilting its head with a soft mechanical click. As it did so, they could see its face for the first time. It stared at them with lifeless eyes, simple glass beads encased by a mask that was frozen in a spine-chilling grin.

Dorian gulped. Irene and her mother took a step

back. The figure stretched out one hand and then stood still again.

'I hope Christian didn't frighten you. He's a rather clumsy old creation of mine.'

The Sauvelles turned towards the voice that came from the foot of the marble stairs. A kind face which was aging gracefully was smiling up at them mischievously. Blue eyes sparkled beneath a thick, silvery mop of well-groomed hair. The man, who was elegantly dressed and held an ebony walking stick with coloured inlays, climbed the steps towards them then bowed politely.

'My name is Lazarus Jann, and I think I owe you an apology.'

His voice was warm and comforting. His large blue eyes scrutinised each member of the family until finally they came to rest on Simone's face.

'I was taking my usual evening walk through the forest and was delayed. Madame Sauvelle, I believe . . .?'

'It's a pleasure to meet you, sir.'

'Please call me Lazarus.'

Simone nodded. 'This is my daughter Irene,' she said. 'And this is Dorian, the youngest in the family,'

Lazarus Jann shook their hands courteously. His grasp was firm and pleasant, his smile infectious.

'Right. As for Christian, don't let him frighten you. I keep him as a souvenir of my first period. He's awkward and doesn't look very friendly, I know.'

'Is he a machine?' asked Dorian quickly. He was fascinated.

Simone's scolding look came too late. Lazarus smiled at Dorian.

'You could call him that. Technically, Christian is what is known as an automaton.'

'Did you build him, sir?'

'Dorian,' his mother reproached him.

Lazarus smiled again. The boy's curiosity didn't seem to bother him in the least.

'Yes. I built him and many more besides. That is, or rather was, my profession. But I think dinner is ready. Shall we discuss this, and get to know each other better, over a nice plate of food?'

The smell of a delicious roast wafted towards them.

Neither the alarming reception by the automaton nor the impressive exterior of Cravenmoore could have prepared the Sauvelles for the interior of Lazarus Jann's mansion. No sooner had they stepped through the front door than they were submerged in a world of fantasy far beyond anything they could have imagined.

A sumptuous staircase seemed to spiral towards infinity. Looking up, the Sauvelles could see it vanishing towards the central tower of Cravenmoore, which was crowned by a small turret with windows all around, infusing the house with an other-worldly light. Beneath this spectral glow lay an immense gallery of mechanical creations. On one of the walls, a large clock with cartoon eyes smiled at the visitors. A ballerina, wrapped in a transparent veil, pirouetted in the centre of an oval hall in which every object, every detail, formed part of the world of fantastical creatures brought to life by Lazarus Jann. The doorknobs were smiling faces that winked as you turned them. A large owl with magnificent plumage slowly dilated its glass pupils as it flapped its wings. Dozens, perhaps hundreds, of miniature figures and toys filled an endless array of display cabinets it would have taken a whole lifetime to explore. A small mechanical puppy wagged its tail and barked playfully as a tiny metal mouse scurried by. Hanging from the ceiling, a merry-go-round of dragons and stars danced in mid-air to the distant notes of a music box.

Wherever they looked, the Sauvelles discovered new marvels, impossible new creations that defied anything they had ever seen before. For a few minutes all three of them just stood there, completely bewitched.

'It's . . . it's amazing!' said Irene, unable to believe her eyes.

'Well, this is only the entrance hall. But I'm glad you like it,' said Lazarus, leading them towards Cravenmoore's grand dining room.

Dorian's eyes were as big as saucers. He was speechless. Simone and Irene, who were equally stunned, tried hard not to fall under the spell cast by the house.

The room where dinner was served was no less impressive. From the glassware to the cutlery, the crockery to the rich carpets covering the floor, everything bore the mark of Lazarus Jann. Not one object in the house seemed to belong to the real world, to the drab, horribly mundane world they had left behind the moment they stepped inside the mansion. But Irene's eyes were glued to a large painting that hung above the fireplace, which was shaped like the flaming jaws of a dragon. It was the portrait of a lady wearing a white dress. She was stunningly beautiful. The power of her gaze seemed to transcend the painter's brush and became almost real. For a few seconds, Irene was mesmerised by her strange captivating eyes.

'My wife, Alexandra . . . When she was still in good health. Marvellous days those were,' said Lazarus behind her, his voice tinged with sadness.

The dinner passed pleasantly in the glow of the flames. Lazarus Jann proved to be an excellent host who quickly charmed Dorian and Irene with his jokes and astonishing stories. As the evening wore on, he told them that the delicious food had been prepared by Hannah, a girl of Irene's age who worked for him as a cook and a maid. After the first few minutes, the initial tension lifted and the Sauvelles began to join in the toymaker's relaxed conversation.

By the time they started on the second course (roast turkey, Hannah's speciality) the Sauvelles felt as if they were in the presence of an old friend. Simone was relieved to see that the affection flowing between her children and Lazarus was mutual. Even she was falling for his charm.

Between one anecdote and the next, Lazarus also

gave them polite explanations about the house and the nature of the duties Simone's new job entailed. Friday night was Hannah's night off and she spent it with her family in Blue Bay. But they would get the chance to meet her as soon as she returned to work, Lazarus said. Hannah was the only other person, apart from Lazarus and his wife, who lived at Cravenmoore. She would help the Sauvelles settle in and deal with any queries that might arise concerning the house.

When the dessert arrived – an irresistible raspberry tart – Lazarus began to sketch out what he expected of them. Although he had retired, he still worked occasionally in his workshop, which occupied an adjacent building. Both the factory and the rooms on all floors above ground level were forbidden to them. They must never, under any circumstances, set foot in any of them. Especially in the west wing, as this was where his wife lived.

For over twenty years, Alexandra Jann had been suffering from a strange and incurable disease that confined her to her bed. Lazarus's wife lived on the second floor of the west wing, in a room which only her husband entered in order to look after her and provide her with the care her condition required. The toymaker told them that his wife, then a beautiful young woman, full of life, had caught the mysterious illness while they were travelling around central Europe.

The deadly virus slowly took hold of her and very soon she could barely walk. Within six months her health had deteriorated further, turning her into a complete invalid, a sad reminder of the person he had married only a few years earlier. Twelve months after catching the disease, her memory began to fail and in a matter of weeks she could scarcely recognise her own husband. From that point on she stopped speaking, and looking into her eyes was like gazing into a bottomless well. Alexandra Jann was twenty-six at the time. She had never again left Cravenmoore.

The Sauvelles listened in silence to Lazarus's sad account. Obviously distressed by his memories and the two decades of solitude, he nonetheless tried to play down the matter by shifting the conversation to Hannah's mouth-watering tart. But the sorrow in his eyes did not go unnoticed by Irene.

It wasn't hard for her to imagine why Lazarus Jann had escaped into a place of his own making. Deprived of what he most loved, he had taken refuge in a fantasy world, creating hundreds of creatures with which to fill the deep loneliness surrounding him.

As she listened to the toymaker's words, Irene realised she would no longer be able to view Cravenmoore as the magnificent product of a boundless imagination, the ultimate expression of the genius that had created it. Having learned to recognise the emptiness of her own loss, she knew this place to be little more than the dark reflection of the solitude that had overwhelmed Lazarus during the past twenty years. Every piece of that marvellous world was a silent tear.

By the time they had finished dinner, Simone Sauvelle was quite clear about her obligations and responsibilities. Her duties would be rather like those of a housekeeper, a job that had little to do with her original profession as a teacher. Nevertheless, she was prepared to do her best in order to guarantee a good future for her children. Simone would supervise Hannah's chores and those of the occasional servants; she would be in charge of all administrative work and the maintenance of Lazarus Jann's property; deal with suppliers and shopkeepers; take care of the post; and guarantee that nothing and nobody would intrude on the toymaker's withdrawal from the outside world. Her job also included buying books for Lazarus's library. Her employer had made it clear that her past work as a teacher had been one of the reasons he'd chosen her over other candidates with far greater experience in housekeeping. Lazarus insisted that this was one of her most important responsibilities.

In exchange for her work, Simone and her children would be allowed to live at Seaview and she would receive a more than reasonable salary. Lazarus would take care of Irene and Dorian's school expenses for the following year, at the end of the summer. He also promised to cover the costs of a university degree for both children if they showed the ability and the interest. For their part, Irene and Dorian could help their mother with whatever tasks she assigned them in the mansion, as long as they respected the golden rule: never to exceed the boundaries the owner had laid down for them.

To Simone, considering all the misery of the

previous months, Lazarus's offer seemed like a blessing from heaven. Blue Bay was an idyllic place to start a new life with her children. The job was more than desirable and Lazarus was evidently a kind and generous employer. Sooner or later, luck had to come their way. Fate had sent them to this remote location, and for the first time in a long while Simone was prepared to accept what it was offering her. In fact, if her instincts were correct, and they usually were, she perceived a genuine warmth flowing towards her and her family. It wasn't difficult to imagine that their company and their presence at Cravenmoore could help soothe the immense solitude in which its owner seemed to live.

Dinner ended with a cup of coffee and Lazarus's promise to a stunned Dorian that, if he wished, one day he would initiate him into the mysteries of the construction of automata. The boy's eyes lit up, and for a brief moment Simone and Lazarus's gaze met. Simone recognised in his look a trace of loneliness, a shadow she knew only too well. The toymaker half-closed his eyes and stood up quietly, indicating that the evening was at an end.

He led them towards the front door, stopping every now and then to tell them about some of the amazing objects they saw along the way. Dorian and Irene listened glassy-eyed to his explanations. Shortly before they came to the entrance hall, Lazarus halted in front of what looked like a complex construction made of mirrors and lenses. Without saying a word, he put his arm into a gap between two mirrors. Slowly, the reflection of his hand grew smaller until it vanished. Lazarus smiled.

'You mustn't believe everything you see. The image of reality we perceive with our eyes is only an illusion, an optical effect,' he said. 'Light is a great liar. Here, give me your hand.'

Dorian did as he was told and let the toymaker guide his hand through the passage between the mirrors. The image faded before his very eyes. Dorian turned to Lazarus and gave him a puzzled look.

'Do you know anything about the laws of optics?' the man asked him.

Dorian shook his head.

'Magic is only an extension of physics. Are you good at maths?'

'Not bad, except when it comes to trigonometry . . .'

Lazarus smiled.

'We'll start there then. Fantasy is derived from numbers. That's the trick.'

The boy nodded, although he wasn't quite sure what Lazarus was talking about. Finally, Lazarus showed them the way to the door. It was then that, almost by chance, Dorian thought he witnessed something impossible. As they walked past one of the flickering lamps, their bodies cast shadows against the wall. All of them but one: Lazarus's body left no trace of a shadow, as if his presence were only a mirage.

When Dorian turned round, Lazarus was observing him intently. The boy swallowed hard. The toymaker nipped his cheek in a friendly manner.

'Don't believe everything you see . . .'

Dorian followed his mother and sister out of the house.

'Thanks for everything. Goodnight,' said Simone.

'It's been a pleasure, and I'm not just saying that to be polite,' said Lazarus. He gave them a warm smile and raised a hand in farewell.

The Sauvelles entered the forest shortly before midnight, on their way back to Seaview.

Dorian was quiet, still entranced by memories of Lazarus Jann's house of marvels. Irene also seemed to be in some other world, lost in her thoughts. Simone sighed with relief and thanked God for their good luck.

Just before Cravenmoore's outline disappeared behind them, Simone turned to take a last look. The only light came from a window on the second floor of the west wing. A figure stood, unmoving, behind the curtains. At that precise moment, the light went out and the window was plunged into darkness.

Back in her room, Irene took off the dress her mother had lent her and folded it carefully over the chair. She could hear Simone and Dorian talking in the next room. She turned off the light and lay down on the bed. Blue shadows danced across the ceiling and the murmur of waves breaking against the cliffs caressed the silence; Irene closed her eyes and tried in vain to fall asleep.

It was hard to believe that from that night on she

would never have to see their old Paris apartment again, nor would she have to return to the dance hall to relieve those soldiers of a few coins. She knew that the shadows of the big city couldn't reach her here. She got up and went over to the window.

The lighthouse rose up against the dark night. Irene focused on the small island enveloped in a luminous mist. A sudden light seemed to shine, like the blink of a faraway mirror. Seconds later, the light shone again, then went out. Irene frowned, then noticed that her mother was standing on the porch below. Wrapped in a thick jumper, Simone was quietly gazing out to sea. Irene didn't have to see her face to know that she was crying. They would both take a long time to fall asleep. On their first night at Seaview, after that first step towards what seemed to be a new and happy life, Armand Sauvelle's absence was more painful than ever.

3. BLUE BAY

Of all the dawns in her life, none would ever seem as radiant to Irene as that of 22 June 1937. The ocean glistened beneath a sky so clear she could scarcely have imagined it during the years she'd lived in the city. From her window, she could clearly see the lighthouse as well as the small rocks that stood out in the centre of the bay like the crest of some underwater dragon. The neat row of houses along the seafront, beyond the Englishman's Beach, quivered through the heat haze rising from the docks. If she half-closed her eyes, it seemed like a paradise conjured by Claude Monet, her father's favourite artist.

Irene opened the window and let the salty sea air fill the room. A flock of seagulls nesting on the cliffs turned to observe her with curiosity. Her new neighbours. Not far away, Irene noticed that Dorian had already set himself up in his favourite spot among the rocks. He was probably busy cataloguing his daydreams, his flights of fancy, or whatever it was that engrossed him during his solitary wanderings.

She was trying to make up her mind what to wear when she heard an unfamiliar voice, speaking fast and cheerfully, downstairs. She listened carefully for a couple of seconds and could hear the calm, composed voice of her mother attempting to respond, or rather trying to slip a word or two into the few gaps left by the other person.

As she got dressed, Irene tried to imagine what the owner of the voice would look like. Ever since she was small, that had been one of her favourite things – listening to a voice with her eyes closed and trying to imagine the person it belonged to: deciding on their height, weight, face . . .

This time she imagined a young woman, not very tall, nervous and fidgety, with dark hair, probably dark eyes too. With that portrait in mind Irene set off down the stairs to satisfy both her hunger with a good breakfast and, more importantly, her curiosity.

As soon as she went into the sitting room, she realised her first, and only, mistake: the girl's hair was straw-coloured. As for the rest, she'd been spot on. That is how Irene first met the quirky and chatty young Hannah; not by sight, but by sound.

Simone Sauvelle did her best to repay Hannah for the meal she had prepared for them the night before with a delicious breakfast. The young girl devoured her food even faster than she spoke. The torrent of anecdotes, gossip and stories about the town and its inhabitants, which she reeled off at lightning speed, meant that after only a few minutes of her company Simone and Irene felt as if they'd known Hannah all their lives.

Between bites of toast, Hannah summarised her biography in a few quick instalments. She would be sixteen in November; her parents owned a house in the village; her father was a fisherman and her mother a baker; their cousin Ismael, who'd lost both his parents years ago, also lived with them and helped her father on his boat. She no longer went to school because that old witch Jeanne Brau, the headmistress of the local school, had decided she was thick, or at least not very bright. Ismael, however, was teaching her to read and every week she was getting better at her times tables. Her favourite colour was yellow and she liked collecting shells along the Englishman's Beach. Her favourite pastime was listening to romance serials on the radio and going to the summer dances held in the main square, when travelling bands came to the village. She didn't use perfume, but she loved lipstick . . .

Listening to Hannah was entertaining and exhausting in equal measure. After wolfing down her own breakfast, and Irene's leftovers, she stopped talking for a few seconds. The silence that filled the room felt unreal. It didn't last long, of course.

'Shall we go for a walk so I can show you the village?' she asked, suddenly excited at the prospect of acting as a tourist guide.

Irene and her mother exchanged glances.

'I'd love that,' said Irene after a short pause.

Hannah smiled from ear to ear.

'Don't worry, Madame Sauvelle. I'll bring her back in one piece.'

27

Irene and her new friend shot out through the front door and set off towards the Englishman's Beach, while the house slowly recovered its sense of calm. Simone took her cup of coffee out onto the porch to enjoy the peaceful morning. Dorian waved at her from the cliffs.

Simone waved back at him. Curious boy. Always alone. He didn't seem to be interested in making friends, or perhaps he didn't know how to. Always lost in his own world and his notebooks, and whatever else filled his mind . . . As she finished her coffee, Simone took one last look at Hannah and her daughter walking off towards the village. Hannah was still chatting away. It takes all sorts, she thought.

Learning about the mysteries and subtleties of life in a small coastal village took up most of the Sauvelles' time that first month in Blue Bay. The initial phase – a period characterised by culture shock and confusion – lasted a good week. During that time they discovered that, apart from the metric system, all the customs, rules and peculiarities of Blue Bay were completely different to their Paris equivalents. Firstly, there was the question of timekeeping. In Paris it wouldn't be an exaggeration to say that for every thousand inhabitants there were another thousand watches – tyrannical inventions that organised life with military precision. Yet in Blue Bay there seemed to be no other timepiece than the sun. And no other cars but Doctor Giraud's, the vehicle belonging to the police and Lazarus's car. And no other . . . the list seemed endless. But deep down, the differences didn't lie in the number of things, but in the way of life.

Paris was a city of strangers, a place where you could live for years without knowing the name of the person who lived across the landing. In Blue Bay you couldn't sneeze or scratch the tip of your nose without the event being widely commented on by the whole community. This was a village where even a cold was news and where news was passed on quicker than a cold. There was no local paper, nor was there any need for one.

It was Hannah's mission to instruct the family on the life, history and wonders of the small community. Because of the dizzying speed with which the girl machine-gunned out her words, she managed to compress into a few sessions enough information to fill an encyclopedia. This was how they found out that Laurent Savant, the local priest, organised diving championships and marathons, and that on top of his stammering sermons about laziness and lack of exercise, he'd covered more miles on his bicycle than Marco Polo. They also learned that the village council met on Tuesdays and Thursdays at one o'clock to discuss local issues. During these meetings, Jean-Luc Dupuy, who had effectively been appointed mayor of Blue Bay for life and was as old as Methuselah, spent a good deal of time stroking the cushions of his armchair under the table, convinced that he was exploring the hefty thighs of Antoinette Fabré, the town hall's treasurer and a fierce spinster.

Hannah rattled out an average of six stories per minute. This was not unrelated to the fact that her mother, Elisabet, worked in the bakery, which seemed to double up as an information hub, detective bureau and agony-aunt service for the village.

It did not take long for the Sauvelles to realise that the village financial system tended towards a rather strange twist on Parisian capitalism. The bakery, it would appear, sold baguettes, but in the back room an information exchange was also in operation. Monsieur Desplat, the cobbler, mended belts, zips and the soles of shoes. However, his forte was his double life as an astrologer and tarot card reader . . .

This pattern was repeated over and over again. On the surface, life seemed calm and simple, but underneath it had more twists and turns than the road to hell. The best thing to do was to go with the flow, listen to the villagers and allow them to guide you through all the formalities newcomers had to complete before you could say you lived in Blue Bay.

That is why, every time Simone went to the village to collect the post for Lazarus, she dropped by the bakery to get an update on past, present and future news. The ladies of Blue Bay received her warmly and soon began to bombard her with questions about her enigmatic employer. Lazarus led a secluded life and was seldom seen in the village. That, together with the torrent of books he received every week, had turned him into a source of endless curiosity and suspicion.

'Imagine, Simone, dear friend,' Pascale Sardé, the

chemist's wife, confided in her one day, 'a man all alone – well, practically alone – in that house, with all those books . . .'

Simone would usually smile when faced with such words of wisdom, but never breathed a word. As her late husband had once said, it wasn't worth wasting your time trying to change the world; it was enough not to let the world change you.

She was also learning to respect Lazarus's complex demands concerning his correspondence. His personal letters had to be opened one day after they arrived and answered promptly. Commercial or official post had to be opened the day it arrived, but should only be replied to one week later. And he was adamant that any mail sent from someone called Daniel Hoffmann in Berlin should be handed to him in person, and never, under any circumstances, be opened by her. The reason behind all this was none of her business, Simone concluded. She liked living in Blue Bay and it seemed a fairly healthy place in which to bring up her children. The matter of which day letters should be opened on was something she felt gloriously indifferent about.

For his part, Dorian discovered that even his semi-professional dedication to map making still allowed him time to make a few friends among the village boys. None of them seemed to care whether or not he was a newcomer; or whether or not he was a good swimmer (he wasn't, but his new friends made sure he learned how to stay afloat). He also learned that pétanque was a game only those on their way to retirement played and that running after girls was the domain of petulant fifteen-year-olds at the mercy of hormonal fevers that preyed both on their complexion and their common sense. At his age, apparently, all you were supposed to do was ride around on your bicycle, daydream, and watch the world go by, waiting for the moment when the world would start watching you. And on Sunday afternoons, a visit to the cinema. That is how Dorian discovered a new and unspeakable love, next to which map making and the study of moth-eaten parchments paled in comparison: Greta Garbo. A divine creature whose very name was enough to make him lose his appetite, despite the fact that she was basically an old woman, just past thirty.

While Dorian debated whether his fascination for such an old woman meant there was something seriously wrong with him, it was Irene who bore the full brunt of Hannah's attentions. A list of single, desirable young men was top of Hannah's agenda. Her fear was that if after two weeks in the village Irene didn't begin to flirt, even half-heartedly, with at least one of them, the boys would think she was strange. Hannah was the first to admit that in terms of physical appeal the list of candidates passed the test reasonably well, but when it came to brains they were barely functional. Even so, Irene was never short of admirers, which provoked a healthy envy in her friend.

'If I was as popular as you, I'd be making the most of it!' Hannah would say.

Glancing at the pack of boys milling around nearby,

Irene smiled timidly.

'I'm not sure I feel like it . . . They seem a bit foolish . . .'

'Foolish?' Hannah exploded, annoyed at such a wasted opportunity. 'If you want clever conversation pick up a book!'

'I'll think about that,' Irene laughed.

Hannah shook her head.

'You'll end up like my cousin Ismael,' she warned.

Hannah's cousin Ismael was sixteen and, as Hannah had explained before, he'd been raised by her family after his parents died. He worked on his uncle's fishing boat, but his real passion seemed to be sailing alone on his own boat, a skiff he'd built himself and had christened with a name Hannah could never remember.

'Something Greek, I think . . .'

'And where is he now?' asked Irene.

'Out at sea. He and Dad are aboard the *Estelle*. The summer months are good for the type of fisherman who likes to head off for adventure on the high seas. They won't be back until August,' Hannah explained.

'It must be sad. Having to spend so much time at sea, far from home.'

Hannah shrugged.

'You have to make a living somehow . . .'

'You don't really like working at Cravenmoore, do you?' Irene guessed.

Her friend looked at her in surprise.

'It's none of my business . . . of course,' Irene corrected herself.

'I don't mind you asking,' Hannah said with a smile. 'The truth is, I don't really like it much, no.'

'Because of Lazarus?'

'No. Lazarus is kind and he's been very good to us. When Dad had an accident years ago, involving propellers, he paid for all the expenses of the operation. If it hadn't been for Lazarus . . .'

'So what's the problem?'

'I don't know. It's that place. The machines . . . It's full of all those machines and I feel they're constantly watching you.'

'They're only toys.'

'Try sleeping there one night. The moment you close your eyes, tick-tock, tick-tock . . .'

They looked at one another.

'Tick-tock, tick-tock . . .?'

Hannah gave her an ironic smile.

'Well I might be a coward, but you're going to be a spinster.'

'I love spinsters,' said Irene.

That is how, almost without their noticing, one day and then another went by, and before they knew it August was marching in through the door. With it came the first rain of the summer, passing storms that lasted only a couple of hours. Simone was busy with her work. Irene was getting used to life with Hannah. And as for Dorian, he was learning to dive and drawing imaginary maps of Greta Garbo's secret geography.

Then, one ordinary day, one of those August days

when the night's rain had sculpted towering castles of cloud above the luminous blue sea, Hannah and Irene decided to go for a walk along the Englishman's Beach. It was now a month and a half since the Sauvelles had arrived in Blue Bay and it seemed as if nothing more could surprise them. However the real surprises were only about to begin.

The noon sun revealed a trail of footprints along the white sheet of sand by the water's edge. In the distant port, masts swayed like a mirage. In the middle of a vast expanse of sand, Irene and Hannah sat on the remains of an old boat surrounded by a flock of small blue birds that seemed to be nesting in the pale dunes.

'Why do they call this the Englishman's Beach?' asked Irene, as she scanned the desolate coast between the village and the headland.

'For years, an old English painter lived here, in a hut. The poor man had more debts than paintbrushes. He would give paintings to people in the village in exchange for food and clothes. He died three years ago. He is buried here, on this beach,' Hannah explained.

'If I was given the choice, I'd like to be buried in a place like this.'

'What a cheerful thought,' joked Hannah with just a hint of reproach.

'Don't worry, I'm in no hurry,' Irene added. Just then she noticed a small sailing boat ploughing through the waters of the bay, some hundred metres from the coast.

'Ufff . . .' murmured her friend. 'There he is: the solitary sailor. He hasn't even been back a day and off he goes on his boat again.'

'Who?'

'My father and my cousin arrived back from sea yesterday,' Hannah explained. 'My father is still sleeping, but him . . . he'll never change.'

Irene looked out to sea and watched the boat as it sailed across the bay.

'That's my cousin Ismael. He spends half his life on that boat, at least when he's not working with my father. But he's a good lad . . . See this pendant?'

Hannah showed her a beautiful pendant hanging round her neck on a gold chain: a sun setting on the sea.

'It's a gift from Ismael . . .'

'It's gorgeous,' said Irene, studying the pendant carefully.

Hannah stood up and gave a yell that catapulted the flock of blue birds to the other end of the beach. Moments later, the distant figure at the helm waved and the vessel headed for the beach.

'Whatever you do, don't ask him about his boat,' Hannah warned her. 'And if he brings it up, don't ask him how he made it. He'll spend hours talking about it non-stop.'

'It must run in the family . . .'

Hannah threw her a furious look.

'I think I'll leave you here on the beach, at the mercy of the crabs.'

'I'm sorry.'

'Apology accepted. But if you think I talk a lot, wait till you meet my godmother. The rest of the family seem dumb by comparison.'

'I'll be delighted to meet her.'

'Hah,' replied Hannah, unable to suppress a mocking smile.

Ismael's boat cut cleanly through the breaking waves and the keel sliced into the sand like a blade. The boy hurriedly eased the halyard and lowered the sail to the base of the mast in just a few seconds. He was obviously not lacking in practice. As he jumped ashore, his gaze was drawn towards Irene, examining her from head to toe with the same confidence he displayed in his sailing skills. Hannah rolled her eyes and stuck out her tongue, then proceeded to introduce them.

'Ismael, this is my friend Irene,' she announced. 'But there's no need to eat her alive.'

The boy nudged his cousin with his elbow and stretched out a hand to Irene.

'Hello . . .'

His brief salutation came with a timid, but sincere smile. Irene shook his hand.

'Don't worry, he's not stupid; that's just his way of saying he's pleased to meet you,' Hannah explained.

'My cousin talks so much that sometimes I think she's going to use up the entire dictionary,' Ismael joked. 'I suppose she's already warned you not to ask me about my boat . . .'

'Actually, she hasn't,' Irene replied cautiously.

'Of course not. Hannah thinks that's the only subject I can talk about.'

'You're not bad on fishing nets and rigging either, but when it comes to your boat, cousin, you're on overdrive!'

Irene was amused by the banter between the two cousins. There didn't seem to be any malice in it, just a bit of spice.

'I hear you've moved into Seaview,' said Ismael.

Irene fixed her eyes on the boy and drew her own portrait. Sure enough, he was about sixteen; his skin and hair showed the effects of all the time spent at sea. His strong physique was the result of hard work in the docks, and his arms and hands were marked with small scars – something she didn't often see on the boys in Paris. One scar, longer and more pronounced than the others, extended down his right leg, from above the knee to the ankle. Irene wondered where he'd picked up such a trophy. Finally, she lingered over his eyes, the only feature that struck her as being out of the ordinary. Large and pale, Ismael's eyes seemed to mask secrets behind their intense and somewhat melancholy expression. Irene remembered the same look in the eyes of the nameless soldiers with whom she'd shared a brief dance in time to a fourth-rate band – a look that concealed fear, sorrow or bitterness.

'Have you gone into a trance?' Hannah interrupted her reverie.

'I was just thinking it's getting late. My mother will be worried.'

'Your mother will be delighted to be left in peace for a few hours. But it's up to you,' said Hannah.

'I can take you home on my boat,' Ismael offered. 'Seaview has a small jetty down by the rocks.'

Irene looked at Hannah inquisitively.

'If you say no you'll break his heart. My cousin wouldn't even invite that starlet Carole Lombard onto his boat.'

'You're not coming?' Irene asked, embarrassed.

'I wouldn't get into that tub if you paid me. Besides, it's my day off and tonight there's a dance in the square. Think about it. Some wise words from a fisherman's daughter: all the best matches are made on dry land. Anyway, I don't know what I'm saying. Go on, go with him. And you, sailor boy, my friend had better get home in one piece, do you hear me?'

The boat, which appeared to be called the *Kyaneos* – judging from the name written on the hull – put out to sea, her white sails billowing in the wind as the prow cut through the water towards the headland.

Between tacks, Ismael smiled timidly at Irene and only sat at the helm once the boat was set on a steady course, running with the current. Holding tight onto the bench, Irene felt droplets of salty water landing on her skin in the breeze. By now the sails had caught the wind and Hannah was no more than a tiny speck waving from the shore. The force of the boat powering across the bay and the sound of the waves splashing against the hull made Irene feel like laughing out loud.

'First time?' asked Ismael. 'On a sailing boat, I mean.'

Irene nodded.

'It's different, isn't it?'

She nodded again, smiling, unable to take her eyes off the large scar on Ismael's leg.

'A conger eel,' he explained. 'It's a long story.'

Irene looked up at the silhouette of Cravenmoore looming over the treetops.

'What does the name of your boat mean?'

'It's Greek. *Kyaneos: cyan,*' Ismael replied mysteriously. Seeing that Irene was frowning, he went on: 'The Greeks used this word to describe a dark blue, the colour of the sea. When Homer spoke of the sea he compared its colour to that of a dark wine. That is the word he used: *kyaneos.*'

'So you can talk about other things apart from your boat and your nets?'

'I try.'

'Who taught you?"

'To sail? I taught myself.'

'No, about the Greeks . . .'

'My father was very keen on history. I still have some of his books . . .'

Irene remained silent.

'Hannah must have told you that my parents died.'

She nodded. The small island with the lighthouse came into view, about a hundred metres away. Irene looked at it, fascinated.

'The lighthouse has been shut down for years. Now

everyone uses the new one in the port,' Ismael explained.

'Doesn't anyone go to the island any more?' asked Irene.

Ismael shook his head.

'Why's that?'

'Do you like ghost stories?'

'That depends . . .'

'The people of the village think the island is haunted. They say that a long time ago a woman drowned there. Some people see lights. I suppose every village has its share of gossip, why should this one be any different?'

'Lights?'

'The September lights,' said Ismael as they passed the island to starboard. 'According to the legend, one night towards the end of summer, during the annual masked ball, the villagers saw a woman take a sailing boat from the port and put out to sea. Some say she was going to a secret meeting with her lover on the island; others that she was fleeing from a crime . . . The explanation doesn't matter because in fact nobody could see who she really was – her face was hidden by a mask. But as she crossed the bay, a fierce storm suddenly broke; she lost control of the boat and it was flung against the rocks. The mysterious woman drowned, or at least her body was never recovered. A few days later, the tide washed ashore the battered remains of her mask. Ever since that time, people say that during the last days of summer, in the evening, lights can be seen

41

on the island . . .'

'The woman's spirit . . .'

'Exactly . . . trying to complete her voyage. Or at least that's what people say.'

'And is it true?'

'It's a ghost story. Either you believe it or you don't.'

'Do you believe it?' asked Irene.

'I only believe what I can see.'

'A sceptic.'

'Something like that.'

Irene looked at the island again. Waves crashed against the rocks. The sunlight glinted off the cracked windowpanes of the lighthouse tower, refracting into the ghost of a rainbow that faded away through a curtain of spray.

'Have you ever been there?' she asked.

'On the island?'

Ismael tightened the sails and with a sharp pull of the tiller the boat listed to port and made straight for the headland, cutting across the current.

'How about paying a visit,' he proposed. 'To the island.'

'Can we?'

'We can do anything. It's a question of whether we dare to or not,' Ismael replied with a defiant smile.

Irene kept her eyes fixed on his.

'When?'

'Next Saturday. On my boat.'

'Just us?'

'Just us. Of course, if you're scared . . .'

'I'm not scared,' Irene replied quickly.

'Right then, Saturday it is. I'll pick you up by the jetty, mid-morning.'

Irene turned her head towards the shore. Seaview sat perched above the cliffs. From the porch, Dorian was watching them with ill-concealed curiosity.

'My brother Dorian. Maybe you'd like to come up and meet my mother . . .'

'I'm not very good at family functions.'

'Some other day, then.'

The boat entered the small cove formed by the rocks beneath Seaview. With practised skill, Ismael lowered the sail and let the *Kyaneos* drift in towards the jetty. Then, grabbing the end of a line, he jumped ashore to moor the boat. Once it was secured, Ismael held out a hand to Irene.

'By the way,' she said. 'Homer was blind. How could he have known what colour the sea was?'

Ismael took her hand and helped her up to the jetty.

'One more reason to believe only what you see,' he replied, still holding her hand.

Irene remembered the words spoken by Lazarus during their first evening at Cravenmoore.

'Sometimes our eyes can mislead us.'

'Not mine.'

'Thanks for the lift.'

Ismael nodded, slowly letting go of her hand.

'See you Saturday.'

'See you Saturday.'

Ismael stepped back into the boat, cast off the line and let the boat drift away from the jetty while he hoisted the sail. The wind carried the craft as far as the entrance to the cove; seconds later the *Kyaneos* had sailed out into the bay and was riding the waves.

Irene stood on the jetty, watching the white sail lose itself in the immensity of the bay. A smile was still plastered on her face and a suspicious tingling ran up and down her hands. She knew then that it was going to be a very long week.

4. SECRETS AND SHADOWS

In Blue Bay, calendars only identified two seasons: summer and the rest of the year. During the summer, the people of the village worked ten times as hard, servicing the neighbouring seaside resorts, where tourists and people from the city came in search of sand, sun and expensive forms of boredom. Bakers, craftsmen, tailors, carpenters, builders; all kinds of professions depended on the three long months when the sun smiled upon the coast of Normandy. During those thirteen or fourteen weeks, the inhabitants of Blue Bay worked like busy ants, so that they could then idle away the rest of the year like Aesop's lazy grasshopper and survive the winter. Some of those days were particularly intense, especially the first few in August, when demand rose from practically zero to levels that were sky-high.

One of the few exceptions to this rule was Christian Hupert. Like the other fishing boat skippers in the village, he worked like an ant twelve months of the year. Every summer around the same date, when he saw the other villagers gearing up for action, it occurred to him that perhaps he'd chosen the wrong profession:

maybe it would have been wiser to break with the tradition of seven generations and set himself up as a hotelier, a shopkeeper, or something else. That way, perhaps his daughter Hannah wouldn't have to work as a servant at Cravenmoore and he'd be able to see his wife's face more than thirty minutes a day.

Ismael watched his uncle as they worked together fixing the boat's bilge pump. The fisherman's pensive expression gave him away.

'You could always open a boatyard for repairs and such,' said Ismael.

His uncle replied with what sounded like a croak.

'Or sell the boat and invest in Monsieur Didier's shop. He's been going on about it for six years,' the boy continued.

His uncle stopped what he was doing and observed his nephew. In the thirteen years he'd acted as a surrogate father to the boy, he'd still never managed to erase what he both feared and adored the most in him: his obstinate similarity to his dead father, including a fondness for voicing his opinion when nobody had asked him for advice.

'Perhaps you should be the one to do that,' Christian replied. 'I'm nearly fifty. You can't change your career at my age.'

'Then why are you complaining?'

'Who's complaining?'

Ismael shrugged. They both turned their attention back to the bilge pump.

'Fine. I won't say another word,' Ismael mumbled.

'I'd be so lucky. Tighten that clamping ring.'

'The ring's had it. We should change the pump. One of these days we'll find ourselves in real trouble.'

Hupert gave him the particular smile he reserved for fish merchants, port authorities and simpletons of various sorts.

'This pump belonged to my father. Before that, to my grandfather. And before him . . .'

'That's what I mean,' Ismael cut in. 'It would probably be better off in a museum than on a boat.'

'Amen.'

'I'm right, and you know it.'

With the possible exception of sailing, teasing his uncle was Ismael's favourite pastime.

'I'm not willing to discuss the matter. Full stop. The end.'

In case he hadn't made himself clear enough, Hupert finished off his pronouncement with an energetic and decisive turn of the spanner.

Suddenly a suspicious crunch was heard inside the bilge pump. Hupert smiled at the boy. Two seconds later, the screw of the clamping ring he had just secured was catapulted into the air, arcing above their heads, followed by what looked like a piston, a set of nuts and some unidentifiable pieces of metal. Uncle and nephew followed the flight of the debris until it landed, indiscreetly, on the deck of the neighbouring vessel – Gerard Picaud's boat. Picaud, an ex-boxer who was built like a bull and had the brain of a barnacle, examined the detritus and then looked up at the sky. Hupert and

Ismael looked at one another.

'I don't think we'll notice the difference,' Ismael remarked.

'If I ever need your opinion . . .'

'You'll ask for it. Fine. By the way, I was wondering whether you'd mind if I took next Saturday off. I'd like to do some repair work on my own boat . . .'

'Might these repair works, perchance, be blonde, about five foot five, with green eyes?' Hupert asked casually. He smiled mischievously at his nephew.

'News spreads fast,' said Ismael.

'When it comes to your cousin, news flies, dear nephew. What the lady's name?'

'Irene.'

'I see.'

'There's nothing to see. She's nice, that's all.'

'"She's nice, that's all,"' Hupert echoed, imitating Ismael's indifferent tone.

'OK, forget it. It's not a good idea. I'll work on Saturday,' Ismael snapped.

'We need to clean out the bilge. There's rotten fish in there and it stinks.'

'Fine.'

Hupert burst out laughing.

'You're as stubborn as your father. Do you like the girl or don't you?'

'Mm . . . well . . .'

'Don't give me monosyllables, Romeo. I'm three times your age. Do you like her or don't you?'

Ismael shrugged. His cheeks were as bright as ripe

peaches. Finally he mumbled something unintelligible.

'Translate,' his uncle insisted.

'I said yes, I think so. Although I hardly know her.'

'Good. That's more than I could say the first time I met your aunt. And I swear by heaven above she's a saint.'

'What was she like when she was young?'

'Let's not get started on that or you'll still be cleaning the bilge next Saturday,' Hupert threatened.

Ismael relented and began to gather up his work tools. His uncle watched him as he cleaned the grease off his hands. The last girl his nephew had shown an interest in was someone called Laura, the daughter of a travelling salesman from Bordeaux, and that had been almost two years ago. His nephew's great love, as far as he could tell, seemed to be the sea, and solitude. There must be something special about this girl.

'I'll have the bilge clean before Friday,' Ismael announced.

'It's all yours.'

When uncle and nephew jumped onto the dock and set off for home just before nightfall, their neighbour Picaud was still examining the mysterious pieces of metal that had fallen from the sky, trying to work out whether it was going to rain nuts and bolts that summer or whether heaven was sending him a sign.

By the time August arrived, the Sauvelles felt as if they'd been living in Blue Bay for at least a year. Those who hadn't yet met them knew all about them thanks to the communication skills of both Hannah and her mother, Elisabet Hupert. By some extraordinary alchemy, news seemed to reach the bakery where she worked even before the event. Neither the radio nor the press could compete with Madame Hupert's conveyor belt of croissants and gossip. Which is why, by the time Friday came around, the only inhabitants of Blue Bay who hadn't heard about the supposed love at first sight between Ismael Hupert and Irene Sauvelle were the fish and the interested parties themselves. Little did it matter that nothing had actually taken place; the short voyage from the Englishman's Beach to Seaview had already been set down in the annals of that summer.

Simone, in the meantime, had finally managed to establish a mental map of Cravenmoore, but her list of urgent chores was endless. Just making contact with suppliers in the village, sorting out payments and accounts, and seeing to Lazarus's correspondence consumed every minute of her time. Dorian became her carrier pigeon, thanks to a bicycle Lazarus had kindly given him as a welcome gift. Within a few days, the boy was familiar with every stone and pothole on the road along the Englishman's Beach.

Each morning, Simone began the day by sending off the letters that had to be posted and meticulously sorting out the letters that had come in, just as Lazarus had asked her to. A small note on a folded piece of paper served as a quick reminder of Lazarus's specifications. She would never forget her third day there, when she had been on the point of accidentally opening one of the letters sent from Berlin by Daniel Hoffmann. She only remembered at the very last second not to touch it.

Hoffmann's letters usually arrived every nine days, with almost mathematical precision. The vellum envelopes were always sealed with wax and marked with a stamp in the shape of a D. Simone soon became used to separating them from the rest, and ignored the strange nature of the correspondence. During the first week of August, however, something happened that reawakened her curiosity.

Simone had gone to Lazarus's study first thing in the morning with a few invoices and receipts that had just arrived. She preferred to leave them on his desk early in the day, before the toymaker went to his study, so that she did not have to interrupt him later on. Armand, her late husband, always started his day by going through the bills . . . Until he was no longer able to.

That morning, Simone went into the study as usual and detected a smell of tobacco in the air. She assumed that Lazarus had stayed up late the night before. She was placing the documents on the desk when she noticed that there was something smouldering in the fireplace among the dying coals. Intrigued, she moved closer and prodded the embers with the poker, trying to make out what the object was. At first glance it looked like a wad of paper tied together, but then she noticed

Hoffmann's unmistakable wax seal. Letters. Lazarus had thrown Daniel Hoffmann's letters in the fire. Whatever his motive, Simone told herself, it was none of her business. She put down the poker and walked out of the study, resolved never to pry into her employer's personal affairs.

The sound of rain pattering against the windowpanes woke Hannah up. It was midnight. The room was shrouded in a blue darkness with occasional flashes from a distant storm that cast eerie shadows all around her. She could hear the ticking of one of Lazarus's talking clocks on the wall, the eyes on its smiling face swivelling endlessly from side to side. Hannah sighed. She loathed spending the night at Cravenmoore. It was Friday and she normally spent it with her family, but this week she had agreed to stay at the house.

In daylight, Lazarus Jann's home seemed like a never-ending museum full of wonders and marvels. At night, however, the countless automata, masks and strange creatures seemed to change into a ghostly horde that never slept but remained watching in the shadows, always smiling, their gaze always empty.

Lazarus slept in a room in the west wing, next to his wife's. Apart from them and from Hannah herself, the only other inhabitants of the house were the toymaker's numerous creations, lurking in every corridor and in every room. In the stillness of the night, Hannah thought she could hear their mechanical hearts beating, imagined their eyes shining in the dark . . .

She'd only just closed her eyes when she heard another noise – a regular thud, muffled by the rain. Hannah got up and walked over to the window. Peering out she scanned Cravenmoore's tangle of towers, arches and roofs. The gargoyles' wolfish muzzles spewed rivers of black water out into the void.

The sound reached her again. Hannah now focused on a row of windows on the second floor of the west wing. The wind seemed to have opened one of them; the curtains fluttered in the rain and the shutters were banging repeatedly against the wall. Hannah cursed her bad luck. The very thought of having to go out into the corridor and through the house to the west wing made her blood curdle.

Before fear could prevent her from doing her duty, she put on her dressing gown and slippers. There was no electricity, so she took a candelabra and lit the candles. Their coppery glow formed a spectral halo around her. Hannah placed her hand on the cold doorknob and swallowed. Far away, the shutters were still banging, over and over again. Waiting for her.

She closed the bedroom door behind her and looked down the endless passage that ran away into the shadows. Holding the candlestick up high, she set off on her journey, flanked on either side by the dangling shapes of Lazarus's lethargic toys. Hannah looked straight ahead and quickened her pace. The second floor housed many of Lazarus's older automata, mechanical creatures that moved awkwardly and whose features were often grotesque, even threatening. Almost all of them were shut away in glass cabinets, but sometimes they would suddenly come alive, without warning, commanded at random by some internal device to awake from their mechanical slumber.

Hannah walked past Madame Sarou, the wooden fortune-teller who would shuffle tarot cards with her wrinkled hands, choose one and show it to the spectator. Although she tried hard not to look, Hannah couldn't help glancing at the gypsy's terrifying effigy. Suddenly the fortune-teller's eyes opened and she extended a card towards Hannah. The card showed the figure of a red demon wreathed in flames.

A few metres on, the torso of the masked man swung back and forth. The automaton would peel off one mask after another, never revealing his invisible face. Hannah looked away and hurried on. She'd been down this corridor hundreds of times during the day. They were all just lifeless machines that didn't deserve her attention, let alone her fear.

With this reassuring thought in mind she came to the end of the corridor and turned the corner into the west wing. On one side of the passage stood Maestro Firetti's miniature orchestra. If you put a coin in, the figures in the band would play their own peculiar version of Mozart's 'Turkish March'.

Finally Hannah stopped in front of a huge oak panel. Every door in Cravenmoore had been carved with a different pattern, depicting a famous tale: the Grimm brothers immortalised in the most intricate woodwork. To Hannah's eyes, however, they were, quite simply, sinister. This last room in the corridor was one she had never set foot in. And she wouldn't have gone in now, unless she had to.

She could hear the shutters banging on the other side of the door. Cold night air filtered through the gap between the door and the frame, whispering over her skin. Hannah took one last look down the corridor behind her. The faces in the orchestra stared back through the shadows. She could hear the sound of the rain, like thousands of small spiders scuttling over the roof of Cravenmoore. She took a deep breath and stepped into the room.

An icy gust of wind enveloped her, slamming the door behind her and snuffing out the candles. The sodden net curtains flapped about in the wind like tattered shrouds. Hannah rushed over to close the window, securing the latch the wind had unfastened. She searched her dressing-gown pocket with trembling fingers, pulled out a matchbox and lit the candles once more. The flickering flames lit up the gloom, revealing what looked to be a child's room. A small bed stood next to a desk. Books and a child's clothes laid out on a chair. A pair of shoes neatly lined up under the bed. A minute crucifix hanging from one of the bedposts.

Hannah took a few steps forward. There was something disconcerting about these objects and this furniture, something she couldn't quite put her finger on. Once more she scanned the room. There were no children at Cravenmoore. There never had been. What was the point of this room?

Suddenly, it all became clear. Now she understood what she found so disconcerting. It wasn't the room's tidiness. It wasn't because it was so clean. It was something so simple, so obvious, you wouldn't even notice it. This was a child's room, but there was something missing . . . Toys. There wasn't a single toy.

Hannah raised the candlestick and discovered something else, on one of the walls. Small bits of paper. Clippings. She put the candlestick on the desk and took a closer look. A mosaic of old cuttings and photographs covered the wall. In one of the images was the pale face of a woman. Her features were dark and angular, and her black eyes held an air of menace. The same face appeared in other pictures. Hannah concentrated on a portrait of the mysterious woman holding a baby in her arms.

Hannah's eyes moved along the wall, examining the fragments of old newspapers. There were items about a terrible fire in a Paris factory and the disappearance of someone called Hoffmann during the tragedy. The entire collection, spread out like a row of tombstones, seemed to be imbued with this character's presence. And in the middle of the wall, surrounded by dozens of illegible scraps, was the front page of a newspaper dating back to 1890. On it was the face of a child, his eyes filled with panic, like the eyes of a wounded animal.

Hannah was completely shaken by the image. The boy couldn't have been more than six or seven – and he seemed to have witnessed some horror he could barely comprehend. She felt an intense cold, a numbness, take hold of her as she tried to decipher the text surrounding the image. 'Eight-year-old child discovered after spending a week alone, locked up in a dark basement,' read the caption. Hannah looked at the boy's face again. There was something vaguely familiar about his features, perhaps in his eyes . . .

At that precise moment, Hannah thought she heard the echo of a voice whispering behind her back. She turned round, but there was nobody there. She heaved a sigh of relief. The soft rays of the candles trapped specks of dust floating in the air like a purple haze. She walked over to one of the large windows and wiped away some of the condensation. The forest was submerged in mist. The lights in Lazarus's study, at the end of the west wing, were on, and she could clearly see his profile silhouetted behind the curtains.

Suddenly she heard the voice again, this time clearer and closer. It was whispering her name. Hannah turned to face the dark room and for the first time she noticed the glow coming from a small glass flask. Black as obsidian, it stood in a tiny niche in the wall, yet it was enveloped in ghostly radiance.

The girl slowly moved towards it. At first glance, it looked like a bottle of perfume, but she'd never seen one as beautiful as this, nor had she seen glass so delicately cut. Its stopper formed a prism, casting a rainbow of colours all around it. Hannah felt an irrepressible urge to hold the object and touch the perfect lines of the crystal.

With utmost care, she placed her hands around the flask. It weighed more than she expected and the glass was icy cold, almost painful to touch. She raised it to eye level and tried to look inside but all she could see was an impenetrable blackness. And yet, when she held it against the light, Hannah had the impression that something was moving inside it. A thick black liquid, perhaps a perfume . . .

With trembling hands she clasped the cut-glass stopper. Something stirred inside the flask. Hannah hesitated. But the perfection of the bottle seemed to promise the most exquisite fragrance she could imagine. Slowly, she twisted the stopper. The dark contents stirred again, but she no longer cared. At last, the stopper yielded.

An indescribable sound, like the shriek of pressurised gas escaping, filled the room. In less than a second, the black mass issuing from the mouth of the flask had filled the air, like an ink stain unfurling over water. When she looked at the bottle again, Hannah realised that the glass was now transparent and that, thanks to her, whatever had been lodged inside it had been released. She put the flask back in its place and felt a draught of cold air sweeping across the room, blowing out the candles one by one. As the darkness spread, a new presence emerged through the gloom, a dense form covering the walls like black paint.

A shadow.

Hannah slowly tiptoed backwards towards the door. She placed a trembling hand on the doorknob, then carefully, without taking her eyes off the pool of darkness, she opened the door, ready to sprint away. Something was advancing towards her, she could feel it.

As Hannah left the room, pulling the door towards her, the chain she wore round her neck got caught on one of the carvings. At the same time, a piercing sound echoed behind the closed door. It sounded like the hiss of a large snake. Hannah felt tears of terror sliding down her cheeks. The chain snapped and she heard the pendant fall, freeing her. She turned to face the tunnel of shadows before her. At one end of the corridor, the door leading to the staircase of the rear wing was open. There was that ghostly whistle again. It was closer now. Hannah ran. A few seconds later she heard the doorknob starting to turn behind her. She cried out in panic and hurtled down the stairs.

The descent to the ground floor seemed endless. Hannah was leaping down the stairs three at a time, panting and trying not to lose her balance. By the time she reached the door leading to the back garden her ankles and knees were covered in wounds, but she barely felt any pain. Adrenaline ignited through her veins like gunpowder, urging her on. The back door, which was never used, wouldn't open. Hannah smashed the glass with her elbow and forced the lock from the outside. She didn't feel the cut on her forearm until she reached the shadows of the garden.

As she ran towards the forest, her sweat-drenched clothes clung to her skin in the cool night air. Before taking the path through Cravenmoore wood, Hannah turned to look at the house, expecting to see her pursuer rushing across the garden. There was nothing. Not a trace. She took a deep breath. The cold air burned her throat, searing her lungs. She was about to start running again when she caught sight of a shape clinging to the façade of Cravenmoore. The profile of a face emerged from the darkness as the shadow crept down through the gargoyles like a giant spider.

Hannah threw herself into the dark maze of the forest. The moon shone through the clearings, lending the mist a bluish hue. The wind awoke the whispering voices of thousands of leaves, the trees standing by like petrified ghosts, their branches transformed into threatening claws. She ran desperately towards the light that beckoned at the end of that tunnel, a channel of brightness that seemed to move further away the more she tried to reach it.

A thunderous noise filled the forest. The shadow was ploughing through the undergrowth, destroying everything in its path. A shout froze in Hannah's throat. Her hands, arms and face were covered in cuts from branches and thorns. Exhaustion clouded her senses, and a voice inside told her to give in, to lie down and wait . . . But she had to go on. She had to escape. A few more metres and she would reach the road that lead to the village. There she would find a passing car, someone who would help her. Her salvation was just a few minutes away, beyond the edge of the forest.

The distant lights of a car approaching along the Englishman's Beach swept through the gloom. Hannah straightened up and screamed for help. Behind her, a whirlwind surged through the undergrowth then rose up the trees. Hannah looked up towards the treetops shrouding the face of the moon. Slowly, the shadow unfurled. She was scarcely able to let out one last moan. Then, raining down like a torrent of tar, the shadow swooped on Hannah. She closed her eyes and pictured her mother's smiling face.

Moments later, she felt the cold breath of the shadow on her cheeks.

5. A CASTLE IN THE MIST

Ismael's boat emerged through the veil of sea mist that coated the surface of the bay. Irene and her mother, who was sitting calmly on the porch with a cup of coffee, glanced at one another.

'I don't have to tell you . . .' Simone began.

'You don't have to tell me,' replied Irene.

'When was the last time you and I spoke about men?' her mother asked.

'When I was seven and our neighbour Claude persuaded me to give him my skirt in exchange for his trousers.'

'Cheeky little rascal.'

'He was only five, Mum.'

'If that's what they're like at five, imagine when they're fifteen.'

'Sixteen.'

Simone sighed. Sixteen. My God. Her daughter was planning to run away with an old sea dog.

'So we're talking about an adult.'

'He's only a year and a bit older than me. What does that make me?'

'You're a child.'

Irene smiled patiently at her mother. Simone Sauvelle didn't make a good sergeant major.

'Don't worry, Mum. I know what I'm doing.'

'That's what scares me.'

The boat crossed the entrance to the cove. Ismael shouted a greeting. Simone observed him, one eyebrow raised in alarm.

'Why don't you ask him to come up so you can introduce us?'

'Mum . . .'

Simone nodded. She hadn't expected that ruse to work.

'Is there anything I ought to say?' asked Simone.

Irene gave her a peck on the cheek.

'Just wish me a good day.'

Then, without waiting for a reply, Irene raced down to the jetty. Simone watched her daughter grab hold of the stranger's hand (he didn't look much like a boy to her) and jump onto his boat. When Irene turned to wave at her, her mother forced a smile and waved back. She watched them head out into the bay under a brilliant, reassuring sun. On the porch, a seagull, perhaps another stressed mother, was looking at her with resignation.

'It's not fair,' Simone said to the seagull. 'When they're born nobody ever tells you that they'll end up doing the same things you did when you were young.'

Unaware of such considerations, the bird followed Irene's example and flew away. Simone smiled and got ready to return to Cravenmoore. Hard work conquers all, she told herself.

An easterly wind filled the sails of the *Kyaneos* as she ploughed through the shimmering emerald ripples, with glimpses of the seabed just visible below. Irene, whose only previous experience on board a boat had been the short journey a few days earlier, gazed open-mouthed at the hypnotic beauty of the bay. Far away, the tail of the night's storm rode off towards the horizon. Irene closed her eyes and listened to the sound of the sea.

Once their course was set, there was little for Ismael to do but fix his eyes on Irene, who seemed bewitched by their surroundings. With scientific precision, he began by observing her pale ankles, then slowly moved upwards to the point where her skirt inconveniently covered the tops of her thighs. He then went on to assess the pleasing proportions of her slender torso. This process continued for some time until Ismael's eyes unexpectedly met Irene's and he realised his inspection hadn't gone unnoticed.

'What are you thinking about?' she asked.

'I was thinking about the wind,' he lied. 'It's moving south. That usually happens when there's a storm brewing. I was wondering whether you'd like to go round the headland first. The view is spectacular.'

'Which view?' she asked innocently.

This time there was no doubt, thought Ismael: Irene was teasing him. Ignoring her subtle joke, Ismael guided the boat to the outer edge of the current that flowed past the reef, a mile off the headland. From this point,

Irene could see a vast beach, wild and deserted, extending as far as Mont-Saint-Michel, a castle rising through the mist.

'That's Black Bay,' Ismael explained. 'So called because its waters are much deeper than those of Blue Bay. Blue Bay is shallow, more of a sandbank really, only seven or eight metres deep. A natural harbour.'

The rare beauty of the landscape made the hair on the back of Irene's neck stand on end. She noticed a recess among the rocks, like jaws opening out on to the sea.

'That's the lagoon,' said Ismael. 'It's like an oval cut off from the current and it connects to the sea through a narrow opening. Behind it there's something the locals call the Cave of Bats – do you see the tunnel going into the rock? Apparently, in 1746, a storm drove a pirate ship right into that cave. The remains of the ship, and of the pirates, are said to be still in there.'

Irene looked at him doubtfully. Ismael might be good at captaining his ship, but when it came to lying he was a mere cabin boy.

'It's true,' Ismael explained. 'I sometimes go diving there. The cave goes right inside the rocks.'

'Will you take me there?' asked Irene.

Ismael blushed slightly. That sounded like a commitment.

'There are bats in there. Hence the name,' he warned her.

'I love bats. Little rats on wings,' she remarked, determined to carry on teasing him.

'Whenever you like,' he said, giving in.

Irene smiled warmly. Ismael was utterly thrown by her smile. For a few seconds he couldn't remember whether the wind was blowing from the north or whether a keel was some sort of pastry. And the worst thing was that Irene seemed to have noticed. Time to change course. His hand on the tiller, Ismael turned the boat almost full circle, causing the other side of the mainsail to fill with wind. In doing so, the boat tipped so far over that Irene's hand touched the surface of the sea. A cold tongue. She laughed and let out a shriek. Ismael grinned at her. He still couldn't make out what he saw in this girl, but of one thing he was sure: he couldn't take his eyes off her.

'We're heading for the lighthouse,' he announced.

A few seconds later, riding on the current and with the invisible hand of the wind behind it, the *Kyaneos* slid like an arrow over the reef. Ismael felt Irene clutch his hand. The sailing boat flew along, as if barely skimming the water, leaving behind a chain of white foam. Irene glanced at Ismael and noticed that he was looking at her too. For an instant his eyes were lost in hers and Irene felt him press her hand gently. The world had never seemed so far away.

It was around mid-morning when Simone Sauvelle walked through the double doors of Lazarus Jann's personal library, which occupied an grandiose oval room at the heart of Cravenmoore. A whole universe of books rose in a imposing ornate spiral towards a tinted glass skylight. For a few seconds, Simone stood spellbound. Then suddenly she realised she wasn't alone.

A figure, neatly dressed in a suit, sat at a desk directly below the skylight. When he heard her footsteps, Lazarus turned, closed the book he was consulting – an ancient volume bound in black leather – and smiled kindly at her. It was a warm, contagious smile.

'Ah, Madame Sauvelle. Welcome to my refuge,' he said, standing up.

'I didn't mean to interrupt . . .'

'On the contrary, I'm glad you did,' he continued, 'I wanted to talk to you about some books I need to order from Arthur Feldmar . . .'

'Arthur Feldmar, in London?'

Lazarus's face lit up.

'You know the company?'

'My husband used to buy books there when he travelled. It's in Burlington Arcade.'

'I knew I couldn't have chosen a more suitable person for this job,' said Lazarus, making Simone blush. 'Why don't we talk about it over a cup of coffee?'

Simone nodded shyly. Lazarus smiled again and put the thick volume he was holding back in its place, among hundreds of similar books. As he did so, Simone couldn't help noticing the title, embossed on the spine. A single word, and one she was not familiar with: *Doppelgänger*

Shortly before noon, Irene sighted the island straight ahead of them. Ismael decided to sail round it in order to berth the boat in a small, sheltered inlet. Thanks to Ismael's explanations, Irene was now more familiar with the art of navigation and the elemental physics of the wind. She was able to follow his instructions, and between them they managed to overcome the power of the current and slide the boat through the craggy passage that led to the old jetty.

The island was barely more than a single mass of rock emerging from the waters of the bay. A considerable colony of seagulls nested on it, and some of them eyed the intruders with curiosity. As they sailed in, Irene noticed some old wooden huts ravaged by decades of storms and neglect. The lighthouse itself was a slender tower crowned by a lantern room surrounded by glass prisms. It stood above a small, single-storey building, the former home of the lighthouse keeper.

'Apart from me, the seagulls and a crab or two, no one has been here for years,' said Ismael.

'Don't forget the pirate ghost ship,' joked Irene.

Ismael steered the boat towards the jetty and jumped ashore to secure the bow line. Irene followed. As soon he'd finished mooring the *Kyaneos*, Ismael pulled out a picnic basket prepared for him by his aunt, who was convinced that it was impossible to get to know a young lady on an empty stomach.

'Come with me. If you like ghost stories, this will interest you . . .'

Ismael opened the door of the cottage and gestured

to Irene to go in. As she entered the old house, Irene felt as if she'd suddenly stepped back in time. Everything was veiled in a misty film caused by years of damp. Dozens of books, a variety of objects and pieces of furniture sat exactly as they had been left, as if a phantom had snatched the lighthouse keeper in the middle of the night. Irene looked at Ismael, fascinated.

'Wait till you see the lighthouse.'

He took her hand and led her to the staircase that spiralled up into the tower. Irene felt like an intruder, disturbing this world suspended in time.

'What happened to the lighthouse keeper?'

Ismael paused a moment before replying.

'One night he got on his boat and left the island. He didn't even bother to collect his things.'

'Why would he do something like that?'

'He never said,' Ismael answered.

'Why do *you* think he did it?'

'Because he was scared.'

Irene gulped and looked over her shoulder, expecting to see the ghost of the drowned woman drifting up the spiral staircase behind her, a demonic figure with claws stretched out towards her, a face as white as china and dark circles around her blazing eyes.

'There's nobody here, Irene. Just you and me,' said Ismael.

Irene nodded but she wasn't convinced.

'Only seagulls and crabs . . .'

'Exactly.'

The staircase led to a viewing point on the

lighthouse tower from which you could see the whole of Blue Bay. As they stepped outside the fresh breeze and the brilliant sunlight dispelled the ghostly echoes conjured up inside. Irene took a deep breath, mesmerised by the view.

'Thank you for bringing me here,' she whispered.

Ismael nodded.

'Would you like something to eat?' he said.

The two sat on the edge of the platform, their legs dangling in the air, and began to feast on the delicacies hidden in the basket. Neither was very hungry, but the food kept their hands and their minds busy.

In the distance, Blue Bay slumbered beneath the afternoon sun, oblivious to what was happening on that remote island.

Three cups of coffee and an eternity later, Simone was still sitting with Lazarus. What had begun as a friendly chat had turned into a long conversation about books, travel and the past. After only a few hours, she felt as if she'd known Lazarus all her life. For the first time in months she found herself reliving painful memories of Armand's final days, although she also felt a great sense of relief as she did so. Lazarus listened attentively, maintaining a respectful silence. He knew when to divert the conversation and when to allow her memories to flow.

Simone found it hard to think of Lazarus as her employer – the toymaker seemed more like a friend, a good friend. As the afternoon wore on, she realised, with a mixture of regret and almost childish embarrassment, that in other circumstances, in another life, the strange communion between them might have been the start of something more. The shadows of her widowhood and her past life persisted inside her, however, like the aftermath of a storm. In the same way, the invisible presence of Lazarus's sick wife pervaded the atmosphere at Cravenmoore. Two invisible witnesses in the dark.

Simone could tell that identical thoughts were going through the toymaker's mind. A golden light heralded the sunset, spreading a warm radiance between them. Lazarus and Simone gazed at one another silently.

'Can I ask you a personal question, Lazarus?'

'Of course.'

'Why did you become a toymaker? My late husband was an engineer. In fact, he was quite talented. But your work is extraordinary. I'm not exaggerating – you know the truth better than I do. So why toys?'

Lazarus stood up and slowly walked over to the window, his profile tinted orange by the setting sun.

'It's a long story,' he began. 'When I was a small child, my family lived in the district of Les Gobelins, in Paris. You probably know the area. It used to be poor and full of old, run-down buildings. We lived in a tiny flat in an old block on rue des Gobelins. Part of the frontage was propped up because it kept threatening to collapse, but none of the families living there could afford to move to a better part of the district. How we all managed to fit in the flat – my three brothers and me, my parents and my uncle Luc – is a mystery. But I'm digressing.

'I was a lonely boy. Always had been. Most of the things the other children on my street were interested in bored me, and the things that interested me didn't appeal to them. I'd learned to read – it was a revelation – and most of my friends were books. This might have worried my mother had there not been more pressing problems at home. My mother's idea of a healthy childhood was for me to run around the streets, picking up the habits and opinions of our neighbours. All my father did was sit around waiting for my brothers and me to add another wage to the family.

'Others were not so lucky. In our block there was a boy called Jean Neville. Jean and his widowed mother were cooped up in a tiny apartment on the ground floor, next to the entrance. Jean's father had died years before, from a disease he'd caught in the tile factory where he worked – something to do with the chemicals they used. Apparently it was quite common. I was aware of all this because I was the only friend young Jean had. His mother, Anne, didn't let him venture beyond the building and its inner courtyard. His home was his prison.

'Eight years earlier, Anne Neville had given birth to twin boys in the Saint Christian Hospital. Jean and Philippe. Philippe was stillborn. For those first eight years, Jean had had to shoulder the guilt of having killed his brother at birth. Or at least, that's what he believed. For Anne made sure she reminded Jean, every single day of his life, that his brother had been stillborn because of him; that, had it not been for Jean, her marvellous boy would now be standing in his place. Nothing Jean did or said could win his mother's love.

'Of course, in public Anne Neville behaved affectionately enough. But in that solitary apartment, the reality was very different. Day in, day out, Anne would remind Jean that he was lazy. Bone idle. His school results were dreadful. His character more than doubtful. His movements clumsy. His whole existence, in short, a curse. Philippe, on the other hand, would have been adorable, studious, affectionate . . . everything that Jean could never be.

'It wasn't long before little Jean realised that he should have been the one to die in that gloomy hospital room eight years earlier. He had taken the place of another . . . All the toys Anne had been storing up for years to give to her future son had been thrown into the flames, down in the boiler room, the week after she came back from the hospital so Jean never had a single toy. They were forbidden to him. He didn't deserve them.

'One night Jean woke up screaming after a nightmare. His mother went over to his bed and asked him what was the matter. A terrified Jean confessed that he'd dreamed about a shadow, an evil spirit, pursuing him down an endless tunnel. Anne's reply was decisive: it was a sign. The shadow he'd been dreaming about was the spirit of his dead brother, seeking retribution. He must make more of an effort to be a better son, obey his mother in everything, and not question a single one of her words or actions. Otherwise, the shadow would materialise and carry him off to hell. To reinforce her words Anne then picked up her son and dragged him down to the basement, where she left him alone in the dark for twelve hours, so that he could meditate on what she had said. That was the first time he was locked up.

'One afternoon, a year later, Jean told me about it. I was filled with horror. I wanted to help the boy, to comfort him and try to alleviate some of the misery of his life. The only thing I could think of doing was to take the coins I'd been saving for months in my money box and go down to Monsieur Giradot's toy shop. My budget didn't stretch very far. All I managed to buy was a puppet, a cardboard angel with strings you pulled to make it move. I wrapped it up in shiny paper and, the following day, I waited for Anne Neville to go out shopping. Then I knocked on Jean's door and gave him the parcel. It was a gift, I said. Then I left.

'I didn't see him again for three weeks. I hoped he was enjoying my present, since I wouldn't have any savings to enjoy for a long time. Later, I found out that the cardboard angel survived only a day because his mother found it and burned it. When she asked him who had given it to him, Jean didn't want to implicate me so said he'd made it himself.

'Then one day things went from bad to worse. His mother went berserk and took her son down to the basement again. She locked him in and warned him that this time the shadow was sure to appear to him in the dark and spirit him away for ever.

'Jean Neville spent an entire week down there. His mother had got into a fight in the market at Les Halles and the police had locked her up, with a number of others, in a communal cell. When they let her out, she had wandered around the streets for days.

'On her return, she found the flat empty and the basement door jammed shut. Some neighbours helped her to force it open. There was no sign of Jean anywhere . . .'

Lazarus paused. Simone was silent, waiting for the toymaker to finish his story.

'Nobody ever saw Jean Neville in that district again. Most people imagined that he must have escaped from the basement through a trapdoor and got as far away from his mother as he could. I suppose that is what happened, although if you asked his mother, who was in floods of tears for weeks, even months, over his disappearance, I'm sure she'd have told you that the shadow from his dreams had taken him. As I said earlier, I was probably Jean Neville's only friend. Perhaps it would be fairer to say it was the other way round – he was *my* only friend. Years later, I promised myself I'd do everything in my power not to let any child be deprived of having a toy ever again. Even now I wonder where Jean is, whether he's still alive. I suppose you must think this a strange explanation . . .'

'Not at all,' Simone replied, her face hidden in the

dark.

'It's getting late,' said the toymaker. 'I must go and see my wife.'

Simone nodded.

'Thanks for the company, Madame Sauvelle,' he added, as he quietly left the room.

Simone watched him go, then sighed. Loneliness created strange labyrinths in the mind.

The sun had begun its descent and its light was refracted into flashes of amber and scarlet in the lenses of the lighthouse. The breeze was now fresher and the pale blue sky was streaked with a few solitary clouds drifting along. Irene's head rested lightly on Ismael's shoulder.

Slowly, Ismael put an arm around her. She looked up. Her lips were half open and she trembled imperceptibly. Ismael felt a fluttering in his stomach. Gradually, timidly, their lips moved closer. Irene closed her eyes. Inside Ismael, a voice seemed to whisper, 'It's now or never.' He decided on now. The following ten seconds seemed to last ten years.

Later, when the boundary between them seemed to have dissolved entirely, when every look and every gesture was in a language only they could understand, Irene and Ismael continued to lie there, embracing each other. If they'd had a say in it, they would have remained there, on the lighthouse balcony, until the end of time.

'Where would you like to be in ten years' time?' asked Irene out of the blue.

Ismael thought about it for a moment.

'That's a difficult question . . . I don't know.'

'What would you like to do? Follow in your uncle's footsteps, own the boat?'

'I don't think that would be a good idea.'

'Then what?' she insisted.

'I don't know, I suppose this is stupid . . .'

'What's stupid?'

Ismael fell silent. Irene waited patiently.

'Radio series. I'd like to write series for the radio,' said Ismael after a while.

Irene smiled at him. 'What sort of series?'

Ismael looked at her for a moment. He hadn't spoken about this to anyone and felt as if he was on shaky ground. Perhaps the best thing would be to beat a hasty retreat.

'Mystery series,' he replied at last, hesitantly.

'I thought you didn't believe in mysteries.'

'You don't have to believe in them to write about them,' Ismael replied. 'I've been collecting cuttings about a man called Orson Welles who has worked for the radio. Perhaps I could try to work with him . . .'

'Orson Welles? Never heard of him, but I'm not sure it would be easy to contact him. Have you had any ideas?'

Ismael nodded vaguely.

'You must promise you'll never tell anyone.'

Irene raised her right hand solemnly. Ismael's

attitude seemed a little childish, but she was intrigued.

'Follow me.'

Ismael led her back down to the lighthouse keeper's cottage, then he walked over to a chest that stood in one of the corners. His eyes were shining with excitement.

'The first time I came here I went snorkelling. I discovered the wreckage of a boat – the one used by that woman who is supposed to have drowned twenty years ago. You remember the story I told you?'

'The September lights. The mysterious woman who disappeared during a storm . . .' Irene recited.

'Exactly. Guess what I found among the wreckage?'

'What?'

Ismael put his hand into the chest and pulled out a small leather-bound book that was protected by a metal box no larger than a cigarette case.

'The water has affected some of the pages, but quite a few of the fragments are still legible.'

'It's a book?' asked Irene, fascinated.

'It's no ordinary book,' he explained. 'It's a diary. *Her* diary.'

The *Kyaneos* sailed back to Seaview just before nightfall as the blood-red sphere of the sun slowly sank into the horizon. Irene observed Ismael quietly as he steered the sailing boat. He smiled at her then turned his attention back to the sails, tracking the direction of the wind which was starting to blow from the west.

Before Ismael, Irene had kissed only two other

boys. The first, the brother of one of her school friends, was more of an experiment than anything. She had wanted to know what it felt like. The second one, Gerard, was even more frightened than she was, and the experience hadn't dissipated her fears on the matter. Kissing Ismael had been different. When their lips met she had felt a sort of electric current running through her body. His touch was different too. His smell was different. Everything about him was different.

'What's on your mind?' Ismael asked her, noticing her thoughtful expression.

Irene tried to look secretive, raising an eyebrow.

He shrugged and continued steering the boat towards the headland. A flock of birds escorted them as far as the jetty. The lights from the house danced on the waters of the small cove.

'It's almost dark,' said Irene, sounding slightly worried. 'You'll be all right, won't you?'

Ismael smiled. 'The *Kyaneos* knows her own way back. I'll be fine.'

The boat berthed gently alongside the jetty. The cries of the birds echoed from the cliffs. A dark blue strip was now visible above the horizon, and the moon had appeared between the clouds.

'Well . . . it's getting late,' said Irene.

'Yes . . .'

She jumped ashore.

'I'll take the diary with me. I promise I'll look after it.'

Ismael nodded in response. Irene gave a nervous

giggle.

'Goodnight.'

'Goodnight, Irene.'

Ismael began to cast off. 'I was planning to go to the lagoon tomorrow. If you want to come . . .'

She nodded as the boat edged away.

'I'll pick you up here . . .'

Irene stayed there, watching Ismael leave, until the night had swallowed him and the *Kyaneos* completely. Then, floating on air, she hurried back to Seaview. Her mother was waiting for her on the porch. You didn't need to be a fortune-teller to guess that Simone had seen the whole episode on the jetty.

'How was your day?' Simone asked.

Irene swallowed hard.

Her mother gave her a cheeky smile. 'You can tell me.'

Irene sat down next to her mother, who put an arm around her.

'How was yours?' asked Irene.

Simone let out a sigh, remembering the afternoon spent with Lazarus. She hugged her daughter.

'It was a strange day, Irene. I suppose I'm growing old.'

'What rubbish.'

Irene looked into her mother's eyes.

'Is something wrong, Mum?'

Simone smiled faintly and shook her head.

'I just miss your father,' she replied finally, a tear rolling down her cheek.

'Dad is gone,' said Irene. 'You have to let go of him.'

'I don't know if I want to.'

Irene hugged her mother and could hear the sound of her tears in the darkness.

6. THE DIARY OF ALMA MALTISSE

Dawn crept on Irene almost without her noticing. She was still engrossed in the diary with which Ismael had entrusted her. What had begun as simple curiosity some hours earlier had become an obsession during the night. From the very first line, the faded handwriting of the mysterious woman who had disappeared in the waters of the bay had captured her imagination. After only a few words, she had known she could not go to sleep.

Today, for the first time, I've seen the shadow's face. It was watching me from a dark corner, lying in wait, motionless and silent. I know perfectly well what I saw in those eyes, the force that keeps the shadow alive: hatred. I could feel its presence and I'm certain that, sooner or later, our life in this place will become a nightmare. I've finally understood the help he needs, and, come what may, I cannot leave him on his own . . .

As Irene turned the pages, the woman's voice seemed to be whispering to her, confiding secrets that had remained forgotten for years. Six hours after she had started reading the diary, Irene felt that this stranger had become more like an invisible friend who had chosen her to be the repository of her private thoughts and her memories.

It has happened again. This time it was my clothes. In the morning, when I went to my dressing room, I found the wardrobe door open and all my dresses, the dresses he has given me over the years, shredded to ribbons, as if sliced by the blades of a hundred knives. A week ago it was my engagement ring. I found it lying on the floor, twisted and ruined. Other jewels have disappeared. The mirrors in my room are cracked. Every day its presence is stronger and its anger more palpable. It's just a matter of time before the attacks stop focusing on my possessions and turn on me instead. I'm the one it hates. I'm the one it wants to kill. There's not enough room for both of us in this place . . .

Sunlight flooded her room as Irene turned the last page of the diary. For a moment it occurred to her that she'd never known as much about anyone. Nobody, not even her own mother had disclosed the very secrets of her soul as candidly as this woman who she'd never met. A woman who had died years before she was born.

I have nobody to talk to, nobody in whom I can confide the horror that invades my soul day after day. Sometimes I wish I could turn back, retrace my steps. But that is when I realise most clearly that my fear and sorrow cannot compare to his, that he needs me and that, without me, his light will go out for ever. I only ask that God will give us the strength to survive, to escape beyond the reach of the shadow that hovers over us. I feel as if every line I write in this diary might be the last one.

For some reason Irene felt tears spilling down her cheeks as she thought about this poor woman's plight. As for her identity, all the diary revealed was two words on the top of the first page: '*Alma Maltissé*'.

It was not long after that Irene saw the sail of the *Kyaneos* heading towards Seaview. She picked up the diary and tiptoed off to meet Ismael.

It seemed only minutes before the boat was sailing through the choppy current that flowed around the tip of the headland and had entered Black Bay. The morning light sculpted silhouettes along the cliffs that made up much of the coastline, great walls of rock confronting the ocean. At the helm, Ismael seemed unusually cheerful as he steered the boat towards the lagoon. Happy to be under the spell of the sea, Irene told him what she had discovered through reading Alma Maltisse's diary.

'She obviously wrote it for herself,' she explained. 'But it's strange that she never mentions anyone by name. The people seem to be invisible.'

'It's impenetrable,' said Ismael, who had given up trying to read the diary long ago.

'Not at all,' Irene objected. 'The thing is, you have to be a woman to understand it.'

Ismael pursed his lips and was about to fire off a quick reply, but for some reason, he thought twice about it.

Before long, the wind had carried them to the entrance of the lagoon – a narrow passage between the rocks leading to a natural harbour. Inside it the water, only three or four metres deep, sparkled above the sandy white swathe of the seabed. Irene gazed in amazement at the scene as a shoal of silver fish darted beneath the hull of the *Kyaneos*.

'It's incredible,' she spluttered.

'It's the lagoon,' Ismael countered, his tone more prosaic.

While Irene drank in the view, Ismael lowered the sails and dropped anchor. The *Kyaneos* swayed gently, like a leaf on a calm pond.

'Right. Do you want to see this cave, or don't you?'

Smiling defiantly, without taking her eyes off Ismael's, Irene slowly removed her dress. Ismael could do nothing but stare. Clad in a skimpy swimsuit, so skimpy her mother would never have called it by that name, Irene grinned at Ismael's reaction. After letting him admire her in stunned silence for a couple of seconds, but not long enough for him to get used to it, she plunged into the shimmering sea. Ismael gulped.

Either he was very slow or this girl was too fast for him. Without wasting another moment, he dived in after her.

Ismael and Irene swam towards the entrance of the Cave of Bats. The tunnel burrowed into the land like a cathedral gouged out of rock. The cave had a vaulted ceiling, crowned by large shards of rock that dangled down into the void like tears of ice. Sunlight glinted through cracks, revealing a thousand and one nooks and crannies among the rocks. In the half light the sandy seabed emitted a ghostly phosphorescence that spread like a luminous carpet towards the interior of the cave.

Irene submerged herself beneath the water and opened her eyes. A world of fleeting reflections danced before her, inhabited by creatures both strange and fascinating. Small fish whose scales changed colour depending on how the light fell; iridescent plants clinging to the rocks; minute crabs scuttling around the seabed. She gazed at the undersea fauna until she had to come up for air.

'Keep doing that and you'll grow a tail, like a mermaid,' said Ismael.

She winked at him, then kissed him in the dim light.

'Perhaps I already am a mermaid,' she whispered, swimming further inside the cave.

Ismael exchanged glances with a crab that was observing him with mild interest from its lair on the rocky wall.

"What?" he prompted.

The crustacean seemed to be smiling at his expense.

She's been absent for a whole day, thought Simone. The hours had gone by and still Hannah hadn't appeared. Simone wondered whether this was just a disciplinary problem. She hoped so. She'd spent the whole day waiting to hear from the girl, imagining she'd had to go home for some reason. Some minor ailment. An unexpected family engagement. Come to think of it, hadn't she spent Saturday with her family too, as she hadn't appeared up at the house then? Any explanation would have been enough for Simone. Finally, she decided to face the problem. She was about to pick up the phone and call Hannah's house when an incoming call got in ahead of her. She didn't recognise the voice, and the way its owner identified himself did little to reassure her.

'Good afternoon, Madame Sauvelle. My name is Henri Faure, I'm superintendent at the Blue Bay police station,' he announced.

A tense silence travelled down the line.

'Madame?' said the policeman.

'I'm listening.'

'This isn't easy for me to say . . .'

Dorian had finished his work as a messenger for the day. The errands Simone had entrusted him with had all been done, and the prospect of a free afternoon was refreshing. When he reached Seaview, Simone hadn't yet returned from Cravenmoore and his sister Irene was probably out and about with that boyfriend she'd found for herself. After downing a couple of glasses of cold milk, the absence of women in the house began to disconcert Dorian. He'd become so used to them that, when they weren't around, the silence was worrying.

Since there were still a few hours of daylight left, Dorian decided to explore Cravenmoore's forest. With the sun overhead, just as Simone had said, the sinister shapes revealed themselves to be nothing more than trees, bushes and undergrowth. With this in mind Dorian set off towards the heart of the labyrinthine wood that stretched between Seaview and the mansion of Lazarus Jann.

He'd been walking for about ten minutes when he noticed a trail of footprints entering the forest from the direction of the cliff and then vanishing mysteriously when they reached a clearing. He knelt down and put his fingers in the imprints, which were deep, more like random holes stamped into the ground. Whoever or whatever had left those prints must have been very heavy. Dorian took a closer look at the tracks, following the marks up to the point at which they disappeared. If he believed what he was seeing, whoever had made them had stopped walking and simply evaporated.

He looked up at the web of light and shade spun between the treetops. One of Lazarus's birds fluttered through the branches. Dorian couldn't help shivering. Were there no real animals living in this forest? The only ones he had seen were the mechanical creatures that appeared and disappeared in the shadows, making it impossible to work out where they had come from or where they were heading. He continued to search the area and noticed a deep notch in a nearby tree. Dorian moved closer. Similar lacerations scored the trunk the whole way up to the top. The boy swallowed nervously and decided to get out of there as fast as his legs would carry him.

Ismael led Irene to a small flat rock that jutted out about half a metre in the middle of the cave, and they both lay down to rest for a while. The light coming in through the entrance cast a flickering pattern of shadows against the walls and curved ceiling. The water was warmer here than in the open sea and the air felt almost humid.

'Are there any other entrances to this cave?' asked Irene.

'There is one other one, but it's dangerous. The only safe way in and out is by sea, from the lagoon.'

Irene gazed at the eerie light infiltrating the very depths of the cave. For an instant, she felt as though she were inside the grand hall of a palace carved into the cliffs.

'It's . . . unreal, like something out of a dream.'

Ismael nodded in agreement.

'Sometimes I come here and spend hours just sitting on the rocks, watching the light change under the water. It's my sanctuary . . .'

'Far from the world?'

'As far as you can imagine.'

'You don't like people much, do you?'

'Depends which people you're talking about,' he replied, a smile on his lips.

'Is that a compliment?'

'Perhaps.'

The boy looked away and inspected the mouth of the cave.

'We'd better leave now, the tide will be coming in soon.'

'And?'

'When the tide rises, the cave begins to fill with water, right up to the roof. It's a death trap. You could get caught in here and drown like a rat.'

Suddenly the place no longer seemed magical, but threatening. Irene imagined the cave filling with water, no possible escape.

'There's no hurry . . .' Ismael explained.

But Irene had already dived in and begun to swim towards the entrance. She didn't stop until the sun was beating down on her again. Ismael watched her go and smiled to himself. The girl had guts.

They made the journey back in silence. The words of the diary kept going through Irene's mind like an echo that refused to fade. A thick bank of clouds had spread across the sky, masking the sun and turning the sea a leaden, metallic colour. The wind was fresher now so Irene put on her dress again. This time Ismael barely looked at her as she was dressing, too wrapped up in his own thoughts.

The *Kyaneos* rounded the headland by mid-afternoon and set a course for the cove beneath the

Sauvelles' house. Ismael steered the boat towards the jetty and berthed it with his usual skill, although his mind seemed to be miles away.

When the moment came to say goodbye, Irene took Ismael's hand in hers.

'Thanks for taking me to the cave.'

'You're always thanking me and I don't know what for . . . Thank you, for coming.'

Irene wanted to ask him when they would meet again, but her instinct advised her not to. Ismael untied the line and the *Kyaneos* drifted off.

As she watched him leave, Irene paused on the stone stairway that led up the cliffs. A flock of seagulls was escorting him towards the port. She turned and continued up the steps, a secret smile on her lips.

The moment she set foot inside the house Irene noticed something was wrong. Everything was too tidy, too calm, too quiet. The lights in the sitting room on the ground floor were on and Dorian was sitting in one of the armchairs, staring at the fireplace. Simone was gazing at the sea from the kitchen window, a cup of cold coffee in her hands. The only sound was the murmur of the wind as it gently turned the weathervane on the roof.

Dorian and his sister looked at one another then Irene went over to her mother and put a hand on her shoulder. When Simone Sauvelle turned around, there were tears in her eyes.

'What's happened, Mum?'

Her mother hugged her. Irene clasped her mother's hands in her own. They were cold.

'It's Hannah,' whispered Simone.

A long silence. The wind scratched at the shutters.

'She's dead.'

7. A PATH OF SHADOWS

As Irene pedalled towards the village on her brother's bicycle the sun was setting. For a moment she looked back over her shoulder at Seaview. Simone's words and the alarm in her eyes as she saw her daughter rush out of the house weighed heavily on Irene, but the thought of Ismael sailing towards the news of Hannah's death distressed her even more.

Simone had explained that, only a few hours earlier, two ramblers had discovered Hannah's body near the forest. From that moment on, all those who'd been lucky enough to have known her had been overcome by grief and desolation. There'd been a lot of talk. People were saying that her mother, Elisabet, had suffered a nervous breakdown when she heard the news, and was still under sedation. But little else was known.

Rumours concerning a series of crimes that had upset village life years ago now resurfaced. There were those who saw this new tragedy as the continuation of a gruesome series of unsolved murders that had taken place in Cravenmoore forest during the 1920s. Others preferred to wait until they knew more details of the circumstances surrounding Hannah's death. But the rumour mill didn't throw any light on how she might have died. The two ramblers who had stumbled on the body were still giving evidence at the police station, and two pathologists from La Roche were on their way – or so people said. Beyond that, Hannah's death was a mystery.

Cycling as fast as she could, Irene reached the village just as the sun finally dipped below the horizon. The place was almost deserted and the few people who were out on the streets walked in silence. She left the bicycle leaning against an old lamppost by the entrance to the side street in which Ismael's aunt and uncle lived. Their home was a humble, unpretentious building, a fisherman's house near the bay. It was clear that the last coat of paint had been applied decades ago, and the light of two oil lamps accentuated the effects of the sea air on the façade.

With her stomach in knots, Irene approached the front door. She was afraid. What right did she have to disturb the grieving family at a moment like this? What was she thinking of?

She stopped for a moment, unable to advance or retreat, caught between her reluctance to call and the need to see Ismael, to be close to him at such a moment. At that very instant the door of the house opened and the rotund figure of Doctor Giraud, the local physician, emerged into the street. The doctor's eyes glinted behind his spectacles in the dim light.

'You're Madame Sauvelle's daughter, aren't you?'

She nodded.

'If you've come to see Ismael, he's not at home. When he heard the news about his cousin he got on his boat and sailed off somewhere.'

The doctor saw Irene's face grow pale.

'He's a good sailor. He'll be back.'

Irene walked to the end of the quay. In the moonlight, she could see the lonely silhouette of the *Kyaneos* cutting through the mist as it headed towards the lighthouse island. Irene felt like jumping onto a boat and following him into his secret world, but she knew that there was no point.

The full impact of the news was beginning to sink into her own mind, and her eyes filled with tears. When the *Kyaneos* finally melted into the darkness, she got onto her bicycle again and started pedalling back home.

Dinner was brief that night and silence ruled as the Sauvelles pretended to eat something before retiring to bed. By eleven o'clock there wasn't a soul to be seen downstairs and only one light still burned in the entire house: the lamp on Dorian's bedside table.

A cold breeze wafted in through the open window. Lying on his bed, Dorian listened to the eerie sounds of the forest. Shortly before midnight, he turned off the light and walked over to the window. In the woodland, a sea of dark leaves stirred in the wind. Dorian could sense a presence lurking in the dark.

Beyond the trees stood the sinuous outline of Cravenmoore. Suddenly a flickering glow appeared amid the vegetation. Lights in the forest. A lamp or a torch shining through the trees. Dorian gasped. The trail of small flashes appeared and disappeared as if someone were walking in circles through the forest.

A minute later, wearing a thick jumper and his leather boots, Dorian tiptoed down the stairs and carefully opened the door to the porch. It was a cold night, and down below the sea roared in the darkness. His eyes followed the path lit by the moon, a sliver of silver snaking into the wood. A fluttering in his stomach reminded of the warm safety of his room. Dorian sighed.

When he reached the entrance to the forest, the pale lights had receded into pinpricks barely visible through the mist. Dorian put one foot in front of the other and, before he knew it, the shadows of the forest had engulfed him. Behind him, Seaview seemed very far away.

Nothing could have induced Irene to fall asleep that night. Finally, around midnight, she gave up trying and switched on the small lamp on her bedside table. Alma Maltisse's diary lay next to the tiny pendant in the shape of a silver angel her father had given her years ago. Irene picked up the diary and opened it again at the first page.

The slanted handwriting welcomed her. Slowly, as her eyes caressed line after line, Irene was drawn once more into the secret world of Alma Maltisse . . .

Last night I heard them quarrelling in the library. He was shouting, begging it to leave him in peace, to abandon the house for ever. He said it had no right to do what it was doing to our lives. I'll never forget the sound of its laughter, like the howl of an animal, full of anger and hatred; the noise sent thousands of books crashing off the shelves throughout the house. Its fury grows with every passing day. From the moment I freed that beast from its prison, it has been gaining in strength.

He stands guard at the foot of my bed every night. He's afraid, I know, that if he leaves me alone for even a moment, the shadow will come and take me. For days now he hasn't told me what is occupying his mind, but there's no need. He hasn't slept in weeks. Every night has become an endless and terrible vigil. He places hundreds of candles all over the house, trying to light every corner, so that there is no refuge in the darkness for the shadow. His face has aged ten years in barely a month.

Sometimes I think it's all my fault; that if I disappeared, the curse would vanish with me. Perhaps that is what I should do, leave him and face my inevitable meeting with the shadow. It's the only way we'll ever find peace. The only thing that stops me is the thought of abandoning him. I couldn't bear it. Without him, nothing makes sense. Neither life nor death . . .

Irene looked up from the diary. The maze of Alma Maltisse's doubts and fears was disconcerting but she couldn't distance herself from it. The line between guilt and the need to survive was as sharp as a poisoned blade. Irene turned off the light. She could not get that image out of her mind. A poisoned blade.

Dorian walked deeper into the forest, following the lights he could see shining through the bushes. It was impossible to tell where they might be coming from. Each footstep sounded like an anguished recrimination. Dorian took a deep breath and reminded himself of his objective: he was not going to leave the forest until he had discovered what was hiding there. That was all there was to it.

He paused at the entrance to the clearing where he'd seen the footprints the day before. The trail was blurred now, almost unrecognisable. He walked over to the slashed tree trunk and put his hand on the cuts. Deep. Vicious. He wondered what kind of animal could have inflicted such damage. Certainly not the kind you want to run into in the middle of the night. Two seconds later, there was a cracking noise behind him – someone was approaching. Someone or something.

Dorian hid in the undergrowth. The needle-sharp prickles of the bushes bit into his skin. He held his breath, praying that whoever was approaching wouldn't hear the hammering of his heart. Soon the flickering lights he had seen in the distance became a steady beam, opening a pathway through the floating patches of mist.

He heard footsteps. Dorian closed his eyes, still as a statue. The footsteps stopped. He was desperate to take a gulp of air, but he felt like holding his breath for the next ten years. Finally, when he thought his lungs were about to burst, two hands pushed aside the branches behind which he was hiding. Dorian's knees turned to jelly. The light from a lamp blinded him. After a moment that seemed endless, the stranger placed the lamp on the ground and knelt down in front of him. The face was vaguely familiar but in his panicked state Dorian didn't recognise who it was. The stranger smiled.

'Let's see. Can you tell me what you're doing out here?' said a kind voice.

Dorian suddenly realised that the person in front of him was Lazarus Jann. Only then did he allow himself to breathe again.

It was a good ten minutes before Dorian's hands stopped shaking, when Lazarus placed a welcome cup of hot chocolate in them. He'd taken Dorian to the outhouse next to the toy factory.

They both sipped their drinks and gazed at one another over their cups.

Lazarus laughed. 'You gave me the fright of my life,

boy.'

'If it's any consolation, that's nothing compared to the fright you gave me,' Dorian replied, as he felt the calming effects of the hot chocolate.

'I don't doubt that,' said Lazarus. 'Now, tell me, what were you doing in the forest?'

'I saw lights.'

'You saw my lamp. Is that why you went into the woods in the middle of the night? Have you forgotten what happened to Hannah?'

Dorian felt as if there was a very large marble in his throat.

'No, sir.'

'Well, don't forget it. It's dangerous to wander around there in the dark. For days I've had a strange feeling that someone is prowling around those woods.'

'Did you see the tracks too?'

'What tracks?'

Dorian told him that he too had sensed a strange presence in the forest. At first he thought he wouldn't be able to come out with his fears, but in Lazarus's company he felt confident enough to speak freely. Lazarus listened attentively to his story, not hiding his surprise and even the occasional smile at the more fantastical elements of his tale.

'You saw a shadow?' Lazarus suddenly asked, his tone serious.

'You don't believe a word I've said.'

'No, I do believe you. At least I'm trying to. You must realise that what you're telling me is rather . . .

peculiar,' said Lazarus.

'But you've seen something too. That's why you were in the wood.'

Lazarus smiled.

'Yes. I thought I saw something, but my impressions are much more vague.'

Dorian downed the remainder of his hot chocolate.

'More?' offered Lazarus.

The boy nodded. He was enjoying the toymaker's company and it was exciting to be sitting sharing a cup of cocoa with him in the middle of the night. Looking around the workshop, Dorian noticed a large, powerful-looking shape on one of the tables, covered with a cloth.

'Are you working on something new?'

Lazarus nodded. 'Would you like to see it?'

Dorian's eyes opened wide.

'Bear in mind that it's an unfinished piece . . .' said Lazarus.

'Is it an automaton?' asked the boy.

'In a way, yes. To be honest, I suppose it's quite an extravagant piece. The idea has been going round in my head for years. In fact, it was first suggested to me by someone of about your age, a long time ago.'

'A friend of yours?'

Lazarus smiled at the memory.

'Ready?' he asked.

Dorian nodded vigorously. Lazarus removed the cloth covering the figure and the boy took a step back in shock.

'It's only a machine, Dorian. Don't let it frighten

you . . .'

Dorian stared at the impressive sight. Lazarus had created a metal angel, a colossus about two metres high, with huge wings. Its chiselled steel face was shrouded by a hood and its hands were enormous, large enough to surround Dorian's head with a single fist.

Lazarus pressed a button at the base of the angel's neck and the creature opened its eyes – two rubies that glowed like burning coals. They were staring straight at him.

Dorian felt his insides twist into a knot.

'Please, stop it . . .' he begged.

Noticing the boy's terror, Lazarus quickly covered the creature again.

Dorian breathed a sigh of relief.

'I'm sorry,' said Lazarus. 'I shouldn't have shown it to you. It's only a machine. Don't let its appearance scare you. It's just a toy.'

Dorian didn't seem convinced.

Lazarus hurried off to pour him another hot chocolate. When he'd drunk half the cup, Dorian looked up at Lazarus and finally seemed to relax.

'What a fright, eh?'

Dorian giggled nervously. 'You must think I'm a coward.'

'On the contrary. Not many people would dare to start searching the woods at midnight after what happened to Hannah.'

'What do *you* think happened?'

Lazarus shrugged. 'Hard to tell. I suppose we'll have

to wait for the police to finish their investigation.'

'Yes, but . . .'

'But . . .?'

'What if there really is something in the forest?'

'The shadow?'

Dorian nodded gravely.

'Have you ever heard of a doppelgänger?' asked Lazarus.

Dorian shook his head.

'It's a German term,' Lazarus explained. 'It's like the shadow of a person which, for some reason, has become separated from its owner. Would you like to hear a strange story?'

'Please . . .'

Lazarus settled in a chair opposite Dorian and closed his eyes briefly, as if he were trying to conjure a long-lost memory.

'A colleague of mine told me this story a long time ago. The year is 1915. The place, the city of Berlin . . .

'Of all the watchmakers in Berlin, none was more conscientious or more of a perfectionist than Hermann Blöcklin. In fact, his fixation with the precision of the mechanisms he created had led him to develop a theory regarding the relationship between time and the speed at which light travels through the universe. Blöcklin spent his life surrounded by watches in the small living quarters at the back of his shop on Oranienburgerstrasse. He was a solitary man. He had no family. No friends. His only companion was an old cat, Salman, who spent hours sitting quietly beside him in his workshop while Blöcklin devoted his time to science. As the years went by, his interest turned into an obsession. It wasn't unusual for him to close his shop for days on end. He would spend twenty-four hours without a break, working on his dream project: the perfect clock, a universal machine for measuring time, perhaps even for capturing it.

'One of those days, in the middle of one of the snowstorms that had been pummelling Berlin for two weeks, the watchmaker received a visit from a distinguished-looking gentleman called Andreas Corelli. Corelli wore an expensive white suit and had long, silvery hair. His eyes were hidden behind two dark lenses. Blöcklin told him that the shop was closed, but Corelli insisted on coming in, saying that he'd travelled a long way with the sole purpose of paying him a visit. Corelli explained that he'd heard about the watchmaker's technical achievements and even described them to him in detail. Blöcklin was intrigued, as he had believed, until that day, that the rest of the world was ignorant of his discoveries.

'Corelli's request intrigued him even more. He wanted Blöcklin to make him a watch, but a special one – its hands were to turn backwards. Corelli explained that the reason behind this commission was that he was suffering from a fatal illness that was going to end his life in a matter of months, so he wanted to possess a watch that would show him the hours, the minutes and the seconds he had left.

'The strange request came with a more than

generous financial reward. Corelli guaranteed to provide Blöcklin with enough funds so that he could work on his research for the rest of his life. In exchange, all he had to do was spend a few weeks creating this device.

'Needless to say, Blöcklin agreed to the deal. He spent the next two weeks working intensively. Blöcklin was still busy in his workshop when Andreas Corelli knocked on his door once more. The watch was ready. Corelli smiled as he examined it, and after praising the watchmaker's skill told him that he'd more than earned his reward. Blöcklin, who was exhausted, confessed that he'd put his entire soul into the project. Corelli nodded in agreement. Then he wound the watch and the mechanism began to turn. He handed Blöcklin a sack of gold coins and bade him goodbye.

'Beside himself with joy, the watchmaker was greedily counting his coins when he noticed his face in the mirror. He looked older, gaunt. He'd been working too hard. Having decided to take a few days off, he went to bed.

'The following day, bright sunlight poured in through the window. Still feeling tired, Blöcklin walked over to the sink to wash his face. When he caught sight of his reflection once more, it sent a shiver down his spine. The night before, when he'd gone to bed, his face had been that of a forty-one-year-old: worn out, exhausted, but still young. Today he saw the image of a man closer to his sixtieth birthday. Terrified, he went out to the park to get some fresh air. When he returned to the shop he looked in the mirror again. An old man was staring back at him. He panicked. As he rushed out into the street he bumped into a neighbour who asked him whether he'd seen Blöcklin, the watchmaker. Hysterical, Hermann fled.

'He spent that evening in the corner of a filthy tavern, surrounded by criminals and other shady characters. Anything rather than being alone. He could feel his skin shrinking by the minute. His bones felt brittle and he was finding it hard to breathe.

'It was almost midnight when a stranger asked whether he could sit down next to him. Blöcklin stared at him. He was a good-looking young man of about twenty. His face did not seem familiar, but he recognised the lenses that covered the man's eyes. Blöcklin's heart missed a beat. Corelli . . .

'Andreas Corelli sat down opposite him and pulled out the watch Blöcklin had created only a few days earlier. The watchmaker, in despair, asked what was happening to him. Why was he growing older with each passing second? Corelli showed him the watch, its hands turning slowly counter-clockwise. Corelli reminded Blöcklin of what he'd said, about putting his whole soul into the watch. That was why, with every minute that went by, his body and soul were progressively ageing.

'Blind with terror, Blöcklin begged Corelli for help. He told him he would do anything he asked if it meant he would recover his youth and his soul. Corelli grinned and asked him whether he was sure of that. The watchmaker reiterated what he'd said: he'd do anything.

'Corelli then said that he was prepared to give Blöcklin back the watch, and his soul along with it, in exchange for something which, in fact, was no use to the watchmaker: his shadow. Disconcerted, Blöcklin asked him whether this was the only price he had to pay, his shadow. Yes, said Corelli. So, again, Blöcklin accepted Corelli's deal.

'Corelli then pulled out a glass flask, removed the top and placed it on the table. In a split second, Blöcklin saw his shadow enter the flask like a whirlwind of vapour. Corelli closed the bottle and, taking his leave of Blöcklin, walked out into the night. As soon as he'd disappeared through the door of the tavern, the hands on the watch Blöcklin was holding began to turn clockwise.

'When Blöcklin arrived home in the small hours, his face was once again that of a young man. The watchmaker heaved a sigh of relief. But another surprise awaited him. His cat, Salman, was nowhere to be seen. Blöcklin looked all over the house and when at last he found it, he was filled with horror. The animal was hanging by its neck from a cable attached to one of the workshop lights. The watchmaker's table had been knocked over and his tools were scattered around the room. It looked as if a tornado had hit the place. But there was something else. Someone had scrawled an incomprehensible word on the wall: "*Nilkcolb*".

'The watchmaker studied the crude writing. It took

him a moment to understand what the word meant. It was his own name, written backwards. Nilkcolb. Blöcklin. A voice whispered behind his back, and when Blöcklin turned around, he found he was standing face to face with a dark reflection of himself, a diabolical mirage bearing his own features.

'Then the watchmaker understood. It was his shadow watching him. His own defiant shadow. He tried to catch it, but the shadow laughed and spread itself across the walls. Blöcklin, terrified, watched as his shadow seized a long knife and ran out through the door, vanishing into the darkness.

'The first crime on Oranienburgerstrasse took place that same night. There were witnesses who declared they'd seen Blöcklin cold-bloodedly stab a soldier who was strolling along the road just before daybreak. The police arrested the watchmaker and interrogated him for hours. The following night, while Blöcklin was still locked up in his prison cell, two new deaths took place. People began to talk about a mysterious murderer who moved through the shadows of the Berlin night. Blöcklin tried to explain to the authorities what was happening, but no one would listen to him. Newspapers speculated about the mysterious assassin who, night after night, managed to escape from his high-security cell and perpetrate the most horrific crimes Berlin had ever witnessed.

'The shadow's reign of terror lasted exactly twenty-five days. The end of the story was as unexpected and inexplicable as its beginning. In the early hours of 12

January 1916, the shadow of Hermann Blöcklin entered the dismal prison where the watchmaker was being held. A prison guard who was keeping watch swore he'd seen Blöcklin struggling with a shadow and stabbing it during the fight. At dawn, the guard who took over from the night watch found Blöcklin dead in his cell, with a wound to his heart.

'A few days later, a stranger called Andreas Corelli offered to cover the cost of Blöcklin's burial in an unmarked grave in Berlin Cemetery. Nobody, except the gravedigger and a strange individual wearing glasses with black lenses, was present at the ceremony.

'The case of the Oranienburgerstrasse murders is still classed as unsolved in the archives of the Berlin Police . . .'

'Wow,' murmured Dorian as Lazarus ended his story. 'And did this really happen?'

The toymaker smiled. 'No. But I knew you'd love the story.'

Dorian looked down into his cup. He realised that Lazarus had made up the tale to make him forget the fright he'd received on seeing the mechanical angel. A clever trick, but a trick all the same. Lazarus patted his shoulder.

'I think it's getting rather late to be playing detectives,' he remarked. 'Come on, I'll walk you home.'

'Promise me you won't say anything to my mother,' Dorian pleaded.

'Only if you promise not to wander around the forest on your own again at night; not until we know what happened to Hannah . . .'

They looked at each other.

'It's a deal.'

Lazarus shook Dorian's hand like a good businessman. Then, smiling enigmatically, the toymaker walked over to a cupboard and pulled out a wooden box. He handed it to Dorian.

'What is it?' asked the boy, intrigued.

'A surprise. Open it.'

Dorian opened the box. In the lamplight he saw a silvery figure the size of his hand. Dorian looked at Lazarus in astonishment.

'Let me show you how it works.'

Lazarus took the figure and placed it on the table. Pressing it lightly with his fingers, the figure unfolded, revealing its shape. An angel, identical to the one Dorian had seen earlier.

'You won't be frightened of it if it's that size, will you?'

Dorian shook his head enthusiastically.

'Then this will be your guardian angel. To protect you from the shadows.'

Lazarus escorted Dorian through the forest, talking to him along the way about the mysteries surrounding the making of automata and other mechanical marvels. To Dorian, the ingenuity of their construction seemed akin to magic. Lazarus appeared to know everything and he had an answer for even the most obscure and difficult questions. By the time they reached the edge of the forest, Dorian was fascinated by his new friend, and proud of him.

'You'll remember our agreement, won't you?' Lazarus whispered. 'No more nocturnal wanderings.'

Dorian shook his head and walked off towards the house. The toymaker didn't leave until the boy was safely back in his bedroom, waving at him from the window. Lazarus waved back and turned towards the dark forest.

Lying on his bed, Dorian still had a smile on his face. All his anxieties seemed to have evaporated. He opened the box and pulled out the mechanical angel Lazarus had given him. It was perfect, eerily beautiful. The mechanism was highly intricate, the product of some arcane and enigmatic science. Dorian set the figure on the floor, at the foot of his bed, and turned off the light. Lazarus was a genius. That was the word. Dorian couldn't get over how many times he'd heard the word being misused, when this time it fitted perfectly. At last he'd met a real genius.

Enthusiasm gave way to drowsiness. Finally Dorian surrendered to exhaustion and allowed his mind to take him on an adventure in which he, the heir to Lazarus's knowledge, invented a machine that trapped shadows, thereby freeing the world from the clutches of an evil organisation.

Dorian was asleep when, all of a sudden, the figure slowly began to spread its wings. The angel tilted its head and raised an arm. Its black eyes, like two obsidian tears, shone in the dark.

8. THE UNKNOWN

Three days went by and still Irene hadn't heard from Ismael. There was no sign of him in the village and his sailing boat wasn't moored in the dock. A storm front was sweeping the coast of Normandy, with heavy clouds hanging over the bay in what looked like a blanket of ash.

In the drizzle, the village streets seemed devoid of life on the morning when Hannah made her final journey to the small hilltop graveyard north-east of Blue Bay. The procession followed her coffin to the gates of the enclosure, then, at the express wish of the family, the burial took place in private. The villagers wandered back home in silence, lost in memories of the dead girl.

As the congregation dispersed, Lazarus offered to drive Simone and her children back to Seaview. It was then that Irene sighted the lonely figure of Ismael, sitting on a tall crag above the cliffs that surrounded the graveyard, gazing out to sea. She exchanged a quick glance with her mother, who nodded and let her go. Lazarus's car set off along the Saint Roland's chapel road while Irene walked up the path leading to the cliffs.

A storm was raging over the sea, igniting cauldrons of lightning on the horizon. Irene found Ismael sitting on a rock, his eyes fixed on the ocean.

'I've missed you,' he said.

She smiled and placed her fingers on his lips.

'I've missed you too,' she whispered.

On their way back to the village, Ismael told Irene where he'd been for the last three days. The moment he'd heard the news, he had sailed off in the *Kyaneos* trying to drown at sea the rage and sorrow that was consuming him. Eventually he moored his boat at the lighthouse island, seeking solitude. As the minutes turned into hours, a single thought invaded his mind: revenge. He would unmask whoever was responsible for the tragedy and make them pay. Dearly. The thirst for retribution seemed to be the only antidote that could lessen his pain.

None of the explanations given by the police satisfied him. He found the secrecy with which the local authorities had conducted the inquest suspicious, to say the least. The following day, just before sunrise, Ismael had decided to start his own investigation. Whatever the cost. That very night, Ismael forced entry and slipped unnoticed into Doctor Giraud's forensic laboratory.

Listening with amazement – and a certain amount of disbelief – Irene heard how, after waiting for Giraud to leave, Ismael had entered the cold half-light of the room and, fighting against the thick stench of formalin, had rifled through the doctor's filing cabinet, searching for the folder relating to Hannah.

For company he had two corpses he'd discovered there, both covered with sheets. They belonged to a couple of divers who'd had the misfortune to be caught by an underwater current in the straight of La Rochelle the previous evening, when they were trying to recover the cargo of a ship that had become stranded on the reef.

Pale as a porcelain doll, Irene listened to Ismael's tale from beginning to end. Once the story moved outdoors, she gave a sigh of relief. Ismael had taken the folder to his boat and had spent two hours trying to wade his way through the jungle of Giraud's jargon.

'How did she die, then?' Irene murmured.

Ismael looked straight into her eyes. His own shone strangely.

'They don't know how, but they do know why. According to the report, the official verdict is heart failure. But in his final analysis Giraud pointed out that, in his opinion, Hannah saw something in the forest that triggered a panic attack.'

Panic. The word echoed through Irene's brain.

'She was found on Sunday, wasn't she?' said Irene. 'Something must have happened that day . . .'

Ismael nodded his head slowly. Or the night before, maybe even the night before that . . .'

Irene looked puzzled.

'Hannah spent Friday night at Cravenmoore. The following day, there was no sign of her either. No one saw her until they found her dead body in the woods,' he added.

'What do you mean?'

'I went to the woods. There are marks. Broken branches. There seems to have been a fight. I think someone followed Hannah from the house.'

'From Cravenmoore?'

Again, Ismael nodded.

'We need to find out what happened the day before her disappearance. That might explain who or what might have followed her through the forest.'

'And how can we do that? I mean the police . . .' said Irene.

'I can think of only one way.'

Irene held his gaze.

'Tonight . . .'

As dusk fell, gaps opened in the bank of storm clouds moving in from the horizon. The shadows lengthened across the bay and the sky grew dark, revealing the almost perfect circle of the waxing moon. Its glow cast a pattern of shadows across Irene's bedroom. For a moment she looked up from Alma Maltisse's diary and gazed at the silvery sphere in the clouds. Soon the circle would be complete and a full moon would shine over Blue Bay, marking the night of the annual masked ball that Hannah had been looking forward to so much. Now, she would never attend it.

It was midnight. In a few minutes' time she would go to her secret meeting with Ismael at the entrance to the forest. The idea of crossing the dark woodland and entering the hidden recesses of Cravenmoore seemed rash to her now. Crazy, in fact. On the other hand, she knew there was no way she could let Ismael down, just as she'd found it impossible not to back him up that afternoon when he'd announced his decision to go to Lazarus Jann's house in search of answers regarding Hannah's death. With her mind in a whirl, Irene returned to Alma Maltisse's diary and took shelter in its pages.

I haven't heard from him in two days. He left suddenly at midnight, convinced that, if he went away from me, the shadow would follow him. He wouldn't tell me where he was going, but I suspect he has taken refuge on the island. He always used to go there in search of peace, and I have a feeling that this time he has returned there, like a terrified child, to confront his nightmare. But his absence has made me question everything I believed until now. The shadow hasn't come back while he's been gone. I've remained locked up in my room for three days, surrounded by lights, candles and oil lamps. There's not a single dark corner anywhere and I've barely been able to sleep.

As I write these words, in the middle of the night, I can see the island and the lighthouse from my window. I can also see a light shining among the rocks. I know it's him, alone, locked in the prison to which he has condemned himself. I can't stay here another hour. If we must face this nightmare, I want us to do so together. And if we are to perish in the attempt, let's do so as one.

I no longer care whether I live another day assailed by this madness. I'm convinced that the shadow will give us no respite. And I can't bear the thought of another week like this one. My conscience is clear and my soul is at peace. The fear of the first days has turned into exhaustion and despair.

Tomorrow, while the villagers celebrate the masked ball in the main square, I'll take a boat from the port and go in search of him. I don't care what the consequences might be. I'm ready to accept them. I'll be content just being by his side, ready to help him until the end. Something inside me tells me that perhaps we still stand a small chance of regaining a normal, happy life. I would not ask for anything more...

The sound of a tiny pebble hitting the windowpane interrupted her reading. Irene closed the book and peered outside. Ismael was waiting for her. As she put on a thick cardigan, the moon slid behind the clouds.

Irene looked at her mother from the top of the stairs.

117

Once again, Simone had fallen asleep in her favourite armchair, facing the French windows that overlooked the bay. A book lay in her lap and her reading glasses had slipped down until they were poised on the end of her nose. From a wooden radio in the corner of the room came the alarming strains of a detective drama. Irene tiptoed past the sleeping Simone, slipped into the kitchen and out into the backyard. The entire operation took only fifteen seconds.

Ismael was waiting for her outside, wearing a short leather jacket, his work trousers and a pair of boots that looked as if they'd been all the way to war and back. The night breeze brought a chill up from the bay and sent ripples through the swaying shadows of the forest.

Irene buttoned up her cardigan and nodded in response to Ismael's silent query. Without saying a word, the two set off along the path that cut through the trees. The rustling of the leaves in the wind muffled the distant murmur of the waves breaking against the cliffs. Irene followed Ismael through the scrub. The face of the moon could only be seen in glimpses through the tangle of clouds riding high over the bay. Halfway there, Irene clutched Ismael's hand and didn't let go of it until the profile of Cravenmoore rose in front of them.

At a sign from him, they stopped and hid behind a large tree that had been mortally wounded by a bolt of lightning. For a few seconds, the moon broke through the curtain of clouds, its light sweeping across the façade of Cravenmoore. The fleeting vision sank into darkness again, and a rectangle of golden light appeared on the ground floor of the mansion. The silhouette of Lazarus Jann could be seen standing on the threshold of the main doorway. The toymaker closed the door behind him, then walked down the steps towards the path that ran along the edge of the woodland.

'It's Lazarus. Every night he goes for a walk in the forest,' whispered Irene.

Ismael nodded, his eyes glued to the figure of the toymaker, who was walking towards the wood, and towards them. Irene gave Ismael a panicked look. The boy let out a sigh and looked anxiously around him. They could hear the sound of Lazarus's footsteps approaching. Ismael grabbed Irene's arm and pushed her inside the dead tree trunk.

'Quickly!' he whispered.

Inside, the trunk smelled strongly of damp and rot. Irene felt an unpleasant tingling in her stomach. Two metres above them, she noticed a line of tiny luminous points. Eyes. She was about to scream when Ismael clamped his hand over her mouth and held it firmly shut.

'They're only bats, for heaven's sake! Don't move!' he hissed as Lazarus passed by.

Ismael wisely kept his gag in place until the footsteps of Cravenmoore's master had faded away inside the forest. The invisible wings of the bats flapped in the dark. Irene felt the air wafting against her face and smelled the sour stench of the animals.

'I thought you weren't afraid of bats,' said Ismael.

'Come on.'

Irene followed him through the garden, heading towards the rear of the house. With every step she took, she kept telling herself that there was nobody inside and that the sensation of being watched was just a figment of her imagination.

They reached the wing connected to Lazarus's old toy factory and stopped in front of the door of what looked like a workshop. Ismael took out a penknife and flicked open the blade. He then inserted the tip of the knife in the lock and carefully touched the mechanism inside.

'Move to one side. I need more light.'

Irene stepped back and peered into the darkness that reigned inside the toy factory. The windowpanes were dulled from years of neglect and it was practically impossible to make out anything inside the building.

'Come on, come on,' Ismael whispered to himself as he continued to work on the lock.

Irene watched him and tried not to listen to the voice inside her warning that it was not a good idea to break into someone else's property. Finally the mechanism yielded with an almost inaudible click. A smile lit up Ismael's face as the door opened a couple of centimetres.

'Piece of cake,' he said.

'Hurry,' said Irene. 'Lazarus won't be away for long.'

Ismael stepped inside. Taking a deep breath, Irene followed him. The atmosphere was thick with dust, which floated in the moonlight. The smell of various chemicals permeated the air. Ismael closed the door behind them and they both turned to face what remained of Lazarus Jann's toy factory.

'I can't see a thing,' mumbled Irene, repressing the urge to leave the place as soon as possible.

'We have to wait for our eyes to get used to the dark. It won't take long,' Ismael replied without much conviction.

The seconds went by, yet the darkness cloaking Lazarus's factory didn't fade. Irene was trying to work out which direction to go in when she noticed a figure rising a few metres away.

A spasm of terror gripped her stomach.

'Ismael, there's someone here . . .' she said, clutching his arm.

Ismael scanned the darkness and held his breath. A figure was suspended in the air, its arms outstretched. It was swinging slightly, like a pendulum, and its long hair snaked over its shoulders. With shaking hands, Ismael felt around in his jacket pocket and pulled out a box of matches. He lit one and for a second they were blinded by the flame. Irene held on to him tightly.

Seconds later, the vision that unfolded sent a wave of intense cold through Irene. Before her, swinging in the flickering light of the match, was her mother's body, hanging from the ceiling, her arms reaching out. Irene thought her knees would give away. Ismael held her.

'Oh God . . .'

The figure slowly turned, revealing the other side of its features. Cables and cogs caught the faint light; the face was divided into two halves and only one of them was finished.

'It's a machine, only a machine,' said Ismael, trying to calm Irene down.

Irene stared at the macabre replica of Simone. Her features. The colour of her eyes, her hair. Every mark on her skin, every line on her face had been reproduced on this expressionless, spine-chilling mask.

'What's going on here?' she murmured.

Ismael pointed to what looked like a door leading into the main house at the other end of the workshop.

'This way,' he said, dragging Irene away from that place and the figure dangling in mid-air.

She followed him, still dazed by the apparition. A moment later, the match Ismael was holding went out and once again they were enveloped in darkness.

As soon as they reached the door leading into Cravenmoore, the carpet of shadow that had spread beneath their feet slowly unfurled behind them, becoming thicker and sliding along the walls like a liquid black shroud. The shadow slithered towards the workshop table and crawled over the white veil covering the mechanical angel Lazarus had shown Dorian the previous night. Slowly, the shadow slipped under the sheet and its vaporous mass penetrated the joints of the metal structure.

The shadow's outline disappeared completely inside the metal body. A layer of frost spread over the

122

mechanical creature, covering it with an icy cobweb. Then, slowly, the angel's eyes opened in the dark, two burning coals glowing underneath the veil.

Little by little, the colossal figure rose and spread its wings. Then it placed both feet on the floor. Its claws gripped the wooden surface, leaving scratches as it went. A curl of smoke from the burnt-out match Ismael had thrown away spiralled into the bluish air. The angel walked through it and was soon lost in the darkness, following Ismael and Irene's steps.

9. THE NIGHT TRANSFIGURED

An insistent drumming wrenched Simone out of a of strange dream in which she was waltzing the night away with her deceased husband Armand in one of Paris's old hotel ballrooms, now decayed and covered in cobwebs. In life Armand had never been a dancer, in fact she doubted there had been a clumsier man in all of Paris, yet somehow he had found his dancing feet in the afterlife.

'Come join me here, Simone,' he whispered in a voice that was not his. He looked at her with eyes that were not his either. 'You'll be happy here, with the others . . .'

'You're not my husband, are you?' she asked.

The stranger in her arms gave her a wolf-like smile.

The sound persisted, and by now Simone was wide awake, the chill of the dream fading away. Someone was tapping gently on the window that overlooked the porch. Simone stood up and recognised Lazarus's smiling face on the other side of the glass. Instantly, she felt herself blush. On her way to the door she glanced at herself in the mirror. You foolish old woman, she thought.

'Good evening, Madame Sauvelle. Perhaps this isn't a good moment . . .' said Lazarus.

'Not at all. I was just . . . Actually, I was reading and fell asleep.'

'That means you should change books.'

'I suppose so. Anyway, do come in, please.'

'I don't want to bother you.'

'Don't be silly. Come in.'

Lazarus nodded politely as he entered. His eyes reconnoitred the place quickly.

'Seaview has never looked so good,' he remarked. 'I must congratulate you.'

'Irene deserves all the credit. She's the one with a talent for decorating. A cup of tea? Coffee?'

'Tea would be perfect, but . . .'

'Say no more. I'd like one too.'

Their eyes met for a second. Lazarus smiled warmly. Simone, suddenly embarrassed, looked down and concentrated on preparing the tea.

'You'll wonder why I'm here,' the toymaker began.

Indeed, thought Simone.

'Every night I go for a walk through the forest to the cliffs. It helps me relax,' said Lazarus.

There was a moment of silence, filled only by the sound of the water heating in the kettle.

'Have you heard about the annual masked ball in Blue Bay, Madame Sauvelle?'

'On the last full moon of August,' Simone recalled.

'That's right. I wondered . . . Well, you must understand you're under no obligation to accept, otherwise I wouldn't ask you. I'm not sure I'm making myself clear . . .'

Lazarus seemed like a nervous schoolboy. Simone was watching him serenely.

'I was just wondering whether you'd like to go with me,' Lazarus concluded at last.

Simone remained silent. Lazarus's smile melted away.

'I'm sorry. I shouldn't have asked . . . Please accept my apologies . . .'

'Do you take sugar?' Simone asked politely.

'Excuse me?'

'Your tea. With or without sugar?'

'Two spoonfuls.'

Simone stirred the sugar in then passed the cup to Lazarus.

'I think I've offended you,' he said.

'No, it's just that I'm not used to being invited out. I'd love to come to the dance with you,' she replied, surprised at her own decision. She had forgotten how comforting it could be to have someone take an interest in her. It felt good, although it also felt as if she was betraying poor Armand.

The conversation continued on the porch of Seaview, beneath the oil lamps which were swaying in the breeze. Seated on the wooden rail, Lazarus gazed at the sea of treetops murmuring in the forest.

Simone studied the toymaker's face.

'I'm glad you feel at home here,' Lazarus remarked. 'How are your children adapting to life in Blue Bay?'

'I can't complain. Quite the opposite. In fact, it appears that Irene is already fooling around with a boy from the village. Someone called Ismael. Do you know him?'

'Ismael . . . of course. He's a good boy, or so I've been told,' said Lazarus rather distantly.

'I hope so. I'm still waiting to be introduced.'

'Young people are like that. Put yourself in their position,' Lazarus ventured.

'I suppose I'm doing what every mother does: making a fool of myself, being overprotective of a daughter who is almost fifteen.'

'It's only natural.'

'I'm not sure she'd agree.'

Lazarus smiled, but didn't comment.

'What else do you know about him?' asked Simone.

'About Ismael? Well . . . not much,' he began. 'I hear he's a good sailor. He's supposed to be quite shy, doesn't have many friends. The truth is, I don't know much about what goes on locally either. But I think you don't need to worry.'

The sound of voices meandered up to his window like the trail of smoke from a smouldering cigarette; it was impossible to ignore. Above the rumble of the sea he could still hear the words spoken by Lazarus and his mother down below; although, for a moment, Dorian wished their conversation had never reached his ears. There was something that worried him in every word, every sentence. Perhaps it was just the thought of listening to his mother chatting to a man who was not his father . . . even if that man was Lazarus, a person Dorian considered to be his friend. Perhaps it was the intimacy that seemed to colour everything they said. Or perhaps, Dorian concluded, it was his own jealousy and his obstinate belief that his mother would never again enjoy an adult conversation with another man. And that was selfish. Selfish and unfair. After all, apart from being his mother, Simone Sauvelle was also a woman in need of friendship and the company of someone other than her children. Any book could have told him that. Dorian considered the theoretical aspect of this way of thinking. On that level, everything seemed fine. The reality, however, was another matter.

Without switching on his bedroom light, Dorian crept closer to the window and peered down at the porch. 'Selfish and, on top of that, a spy,' whispered a voice inside him. Cloaked in the comfortable anonymity of darkness, Dorian could see his mother's shadow projected across the floor of the porch. Lazarus was standing, staring out at the deep black ocean. The curtains that concealed Dorian fluttered in the breeze and instinctively he took a step back. His mother said something he couldn't make out. It was none of his business, he decided, ashamed that he'd been prying.

Dorian was about to move away from the window, when, out of the corner of his eye, he noticed a movement in the dark. Quickly he swung round, all the hairs on the back of his neck on end. The room was buried in shadows, lit only by patches of bluish light that filtered through the curtains. He fumbled around the bedside table, searching for the switch on the lamp. It took his fingers a couple of seconds to locate it. As he pressed the switch, the metal coil inside the light bulb flared briefly, then went out, the sudden glare blinding him for a second. The darkness returned, thicker, like a deep well of black water.

'The bulb's blown,' Dorian said to himself. 'Happens all the time. The metal used to make the filament, tungsten, never lasts long.' He'd learned that at school.

These reassuring thoughts vanished, however, when Dorian noticed the movement in the shadows once more. Or rather, *of* the shadows. A shape seemed to be moving in the dark in front of him. A black, opaque silhouette stopped in the middle of the room. 'It's watching me,' he thought to himself. The shadow now seemed to be advancing towards him. Dorian realised that his knees were shaking from sheer terror.

He took a few steps back until the faint glow from the window enveloped him in a pale halo of light. The shadow paused on the edge of the darkness. Dorian clenched his jaw to stop his teeth from chattering and fought against the desire to close his eyes. Suddenly, he thought he heard someone uttering a few words. It took him a few seconds to realise that he was the one who was speaking. In a firm tone, and without a trace of fear.

'Get out of here,' he ordered, addressing the shadow. 'I said out!'

A spine-chilling sound reached his ears, like the

echo of distant laughter, cruel and malevolent. The shadow's features surfaced like a mirage through the jet-black waters of the gloom. Black and demonic.

'Get out of here,' Dorian heard himself repeating.

The hazy face melted before his eyes and the shadow rushed across the room at great speed, like a cloud of hot gas. As it reached the door, it twisted into a phantom-like spiral that spun through the keyhole, a tornado of darkness sucked out by an invisible force.

Only then did the light bulb go on again, bathing the room in a warm glow. The sudden brightness almost made Dorian scream in panic. He searched every corner of the room, but there was no sign of the apparition he thought he'd seen a few seconds earlier.

Taking a deep breath, Dorian walked over to the door. He placed his hand on the doorknob. The metal was as cold as ice. Arming himself with courage, he opened it and scanned the corridor outside. Nothing.

Gently, he closed the door and returned to the window. Below, Lazarus was saying goodbye to his mother. Just before leaving, the toymaker leaned over and kissed her on the cheek. A brief kiss, just a light brush. Dorian felt his stomach shrink to the size of a pea. A second later, the man looked up from the shadows and smiled at him. Dorian's blood froze.

Lazarus ambled away beneath the moonlight, heading towards the wood, but however hard he tried, Dorian couldn't make out Lazarus's shadow. Moments later, darkness had engulfed him.

After walking down a long passageway that linked the toy factory with the mansion, Ismael and Irene headed deep into the heart of Cravenmoore. In the dead of night Lazarus's residence seemed like a haunted palace, with galleries stretching in all directions and hallways inhabited by dozens of eerie mechanical creatures. From the turret in the centre of the mansion, high above the spiral staircase, came a shower of purple, gold and blue reflections that shimmered like the shifting colours of a kaleidoscope.

To Irene, the motionless figures of the automata and the lifeless faces on the walls made it seem as if a strange spell had once been cast, trapping the souls of Cravenmoore's previous inhabitants. Ismael, whose imagination was more prosaic, saw in them only the reflection of the twisted mind of their creator. Which didn't comfort him in the least; on the contrary, the more they ventured into Lazarus Jann's private domain, the more intense the toymaker's presence seemed to become. His personality was stamped on every obscure detail of the building: from the ceiling, a dome with frescoes depicting scenes from famous stories, down to the floor they were treading on, an endless chessboard that deceived the eye with strange optical illusions. To walk though Cravenmoore was like entering a dream that was both fascinating and terrifying.

Ismael stopped at the foot of a staircase and inspected the circular steps that seemed to vanish into the ether. While he was looking up, Irene noticed that the face of one of Lazarus's clocks, in the shape of a sun, had opened its eyes and was smiling at them. As the hour hand reached midnight, the sphere swivelled round and the sun gave way to a moon that shone with a ghostly light. Its dark glistening eyes moved slowly from side to side.

'Let's go upstairs,' whispered Ismael. 'Hannah's room was on the second floor.'

'There are dozens of rooms there, Ismael. How will we know which was hers?'

'Hannah told me her room was at the end of a corridor, facing the bay.'

Irene didn't think this was very helpful, but she nodded all the same. Ismael seemed as overwhelmed by the place as she was, although he would never have admitted it in a hundred years. They both took one last look at the clock.

'It's midnight. Lazarus will be back soon,' said Irene.

'Let's go.'

The stairs rose in a byzantine spiral that seemed to defy gravity, progressively twisting round on itself like the access route to the dome of a large cathedral. After a dizzying climb, they passed the entrance to the first floor. Ismael grabbed Irene's hand as they continued up the second flight of stairs. The curvature of the staircase became more pronounced now, and the route slowly narrowed into a claustrophobic passage cut in stone.

'Just a bit further,' said Ismael, reading Irene's anguished silence.

What seemed like an eternity later, they escaped

the oppressive tunnel and reached the door leading to the second floor of Cravenmoore. They were now in the main corridor of the east wing. A throng of petrified figures lurked in the dark.

'We'd better separate,' said Ismael.

'What? Are you mad?'

'The good news is you get to decide which end you want to explore,' he offered.

Irene looked to either side. To the east she could see three hooded figures standing round a huge cooking pot: witches. She pointed to the other end.

'They're only machines, Irene,' said Ismael. 'They're not alive.'

'Tell me that in the morning.'

'All right, I'll explore this side. We'll meet back here in a quarter of an hour. If we haven't found anything, we'll leave,' he promised.

She nodded. Ismael handed her his matchbox.

'Just in case.'

Irene put the box in her cardigan pocket then looked up at Ismael. He leaned forward and kissed her gently on the lips.

'Good luck,' he murmured.

Before she'd had a chance to reply, Ismael had set off towards his end of the corridor. 'Good luck,' thought Irene.

As the sound of his footsteps faded behind her, Irene took a deep breath and headed off in the opposite direction. Her part of the corridor split into two at the mansion's central point, the main staircase. Irene peeped over the edge into the abyss. A beam of fractured light plunged vertically from the turret above the dome, piercing the darkness.

From the main staircase, the corridor branched out towards the south and west. The west wing was the only one with a view over the bay, so Irene headed off down the long passage, leaving behind her the comforting brightness that fell from the dome. Suddenly, she noticed a semi-transparent veil stretched across the passage, a gauze curtain beyond which the corridor took on a very different aspect. She couldn't see the shapes of any more mechanical figures lying in wait in the shadows but there was a single letter embroidered on the crown-shaped panel from which the curtain hung. An initial: A.

Irene parted the curtain with her fingertips. A cold breath of air caressed her face and for the first time she noticed that the walls were covered by a complex series of images carved into the wood. From where she stood she could see only three doors: one on either side of the corridor and a third, the largest of the three, at the end, marked with the same initial she'd seen above the gauze curtain.

Irene advanced slowly towards that door. Around her, the wooden reliefs depicted bizarre creatures, an ocean of hieroglyphics she could not decipher. By the time she reached the door at the end, it seemed obvious that Hannah would not have occupied a room there. Yet the enchantment of the place outweighed its sinister atmosphere. She felt as if some invisible presence were floating in the air . . . something almost palpable.

Irene's pulse quickened as she placed a trembling hand on the doorknob. Then something stopped her. A premonition. She could still turn back, find Ismael and run away from the house before Lazarus noticed they'd broken in. The knob turned gently beneath her fingers, sliding against her skin. Irene closed her eyes. She didn't need to go in there. She could retrace her steps. She didn't have to give in to that dream-like spell that seemed to be telling her to open the door and cross the threshold. Irene opened her eyes.

The corridor offered her a way back through the darkness. Irene sighed and, for a moment, her gaze was lost in the shimmering gauze. Just then, the outline of a figure appeared behind the curtain.

'Ismael?' murmured Irene.

The figure stood there for a few moments and then, without a sound, moved back into the shadows.

'Ismael, is that you?'

The slow poison of panic started to pump through her veins. Without taking her eyes off the curtain, Irene opened the door and stepped inside the room. For a split second she was startled by the sapphire-coloured light filtering through the tall, narrow windows. Then, as her pupils grew used to the strange twilight, her hands shaking, she managed to strike one of the matches Ismael had given her. She found herself standing in a palatial room that seemed to be like something straight out of a fairy tale.

An intricate coffered ceiling was inscribed with a whirlwind of fantastical shapes. At one end stood a luxurious four-poster bed with fine golden curtains, and in the middle of the room a marble table held a large chessboard, its pieces made of glass. At the far end Irene spied the cavernous jaws of a fireplace in which red-hot logs were burning. Above the fireplace hung a portrait: a pale face, with the most delicate features imaginable, and the deep, sad eyes of a woman whose beauty was astounding. The woman in the portrait was dressed in a long white robe, and behind her stood the lighthouse on its island in the bay.

Holding the lighted match up high, Irene walked over to the portrait and stood beneath it until the flame burned her fingers. As she licked her wound, the girl noticed a candlestick on a desk. Although she didn't really need it, she lit the candle with another match and was surrounded by a hazy glow. On the desk there was also a leather-bound book, which was open.

Irene recognised the handwriting on the parchment-like paper, although a layer of dust made it difficult to read the words. The girl blew lightly and a cloud of silvery particles spread across the table. She picked up the book and turned to the title page. Holding the book closer to the candle, she read the words inscribed there. Slowly, as her mind began to understand what it all meant, she felt an intense shiver run like an icy needle down her neck.

Alexandra Alma Maltisse
Lazarus Joseph Jann
1915

A splinter of wood crackled in the fire, spewing out small sparks that vanished as they hit the floor. Irene closed the book and put it back on the desk. It was then that she noticed someone watching her from behind the gauzy curtains. A slender figure lay on the bed. A woman. Irene took a few steps towards her. The woman raised a hand.

'Alma?' whispered Irene, terrified by the sound of her own voice.

She crossed the few metres that separated her from the bed and then paused. Her heart was beating fast and her breathing was ragged. Slowly, she started to lift the curtain aside. At that moment a gust of cold air blew through the room, stirring the gossamer veils. Irene turned towards the door. A shadow fell across the floor, like a large pool of ink seeping beneath the door. Then a ghostly sound, full of hatred, seemed to whisper from the dark.

A second later the door was flung open and sent crashing against the wall, almost tearing it off its hinges. A claw with long sharp talons like steel blades emerged from the shadows and Irene began to scream.

Ismael was beginning to think he'd made a mistake in working out where Hannah's room was. When she had described the house to him, he'd devised his own mental map of Cravenmoore, but once inside he was totally disconcerted by the mansion's complicated structure. All the rooms in the wing he'd decided to explore were firmly locked and not one had yielded to his cunning. Time was not looking kindly on his lack of success.

The agreed quarter of an hour had evaporated, and the thought of abandoning the search for the night seemed increasingly tempting. A quick glance at his gloomy surroundings gave Ismael one thousand excuses to leave. He'd already decided it was time to go when he heard Irene's scream echoing through the shadows of Cravenmoore from some remote corner. Ismael felt a shot of adrenaline course through his veins and ran as fast as his legs would carry him towards the other end of the enormous gallery.

Ismael barely noticed the dark shapes sliding past him. He ran through the eerie shaft of light beneath the dome and past the junction of the corridors by the central staircase. The chessboard of floor tiles seemed to stretch as he rushed over it, the passage lengthening before his eyes as if the corridor were galloping towards infinity.

He heard Irene scream again, this time closer. Ismael slipped through the curtain in the hallway and spotted the entrance to the room at the far end of the west wing. Without hesitating, he hurled himself inside, unaware of what awaited him.

The features of a cavernous room unfolded before his eyes in the glow of the crackling fire. He was briefly comforted by the sight of Irene, standing against a large window bathed in blue light, until he read the fear in her eyes. Ismael turned round instinctively and what he saw turned him to stone, paralysing him like the hypnotic dance of a serpent.

From the shadows rose a colossal figure with two large black wings, like the wings of a bat. Or a demon. The angel thrust out its long arms, its dark fingers curled into claws. The steely nails shone like blades before the creature's face, which was hidden beneath a hood.

As Ismael took a step back towards the fireplace, the angel raised its face, revealing its features. This was no simple machine or automaton. Something evil had taken residence inside it, transforming it into some kind of infernal puppet. Struggling against the desire to close his eyes, Ismael grabbed the end of a burning log. He brandished it in front of the angel.

'Walk slowly towards the door,' he whispered to Irene.

But Irene was frozen to the spot and did not react.

'Do as I say,' Ismael ordered sternly.

The tone of his voice roused Irene from her numbed state. Trembling, she nodded and started to walk towards the door. She'd only gone a couple of metres when the angel's face turned towards her, alert, like a predator.

'Don't look at it, keep walking,' commanded Ismael, still waving the log in the angel's face.

Irene took another step. The creature tilted its head

towards her. Taking advantage of the distraction, Ismael struck the angel with the log on the side of its head. The impact unleashed a shower of sparks. Before Ismael could pull the log away, the angel had seized it and crushed it into pieces with its knife-like claws. Ismael could feel the floor shaking beneath his opponent's weight.

'You're just a machine. A stupid pile of metal,' he murmured, trying to ignore the terrifying sight of two scarlet eyes peering out from beneath the angel's hood.

The creature's demonic pupils narrowed into a fine line until they looked like the eyes of a cat. The angel took a step towards him. Ismael glanced at the door. It was over eight metres away. He had no way of escaping, but Irene could.

'When I tell you, start running towards the door, and don't stop until you're outside the house.'

'What are you saying?'

'Don't argue,' insisted Ismael, his eyes still fixed on the angel. 'Run!'

Ismael was trying to work out if he could get to the window and escape by climbing down the rugged façade when something unexpected happened. Instead of running towards the door, Irene also grabbed a burning log from the fire and turned to face the angel.

'Look at me, you disgusting creature,' she shouted, setting fire to the angel's cloak. The shadow hidden inside it gave an angry howl.

Astounded, Ismael leaped towards Irene and knocked her to the ground just before the five blades of the angel's claw attempted to slice her into pieces. The cloak was transformed into a whirlwind of fire. Ismael grabbed Irene's arm and pulled her up. Together they tried to get to the exit, but the angel blocked their way and opened the blazing cloak that enveloped it. A blackened steel structure emerged from the flames.

Without letting go of Irene for a second – to guard against any further attempts at heroism – Ismael dragged her over to the window then hurled one of the chairs against the pane. A shower of glass burst over their heads and the cold night wind blew in. Behind them, they could hear the angel coming closer.

'Quick! Jump onto the window ledge!' he shouted.

'What?' Irene cried in disbelief.

Without pausing to argue, Ismael pushed her outside. Beyond the yawning jaws of the broken glass, Irene was confronted with a vertical drop of almost forty metres. Her heart skipped a beat. She was convinced that in a split second she'd be hurtling into the void, but Ismael didn't loosen his grip. He lifted her up onto a narrow ledge that ran along the façade, then jumped up behind her and urged her on. The wind froze the sweat pouring down his face.

'Don't look down!' he shouted.

They'd only gone about a metre when the angel's claw appeared through the window behind them, tearing at the rocky wall and leaving four scars in the stone. Irene screamed: her feet were shaking and her whole body seemed to sway towards the abyss.

'I can't go on, Ismael. If I take another step, I'll fall.'

'You can, and you will. Go on,' he insisted, grabbing her hand tightly. 'If you fall, we'll fall together.'

Suddenly, a couple of metres further on, another window exploded outwards, hurling thousands of pieces of glass into the air. The angel's talons emerged through the frame and, moments later, the whole body of the creature was clinging to the façade like a spider.

'My God . . .' Irene said, her voice low.

Ismael tried to move back, pulling her with him. The angel crept across the stone, its form almost merging with the devilish faces of the gargoyles that lined the upper reaches of Cravenmoore.

Ismael quickly scanned the scene before them. The creature was getting closer with every step.

'Ismael . . .'

'I know, I know!'

He calculated the possibility of surviving a leap from that height. Zero, and that was being generous. The alternative – going back into the room – would take too long; by the time they had retraced their steps along the ledge, the angel would be upon them. He knew he had only a few seconds left to make a decision. Irene's hand gripped his tightly; she was trembling. Ismael glanced at the angel one last time, as it crawled towards them, slowly but inexorably. He swallowed hard and looked in the other direction. Just below his feet, a drainpipe ran down the outside of the building towards the ground. One half of his brain was wondering whether the structure would bear the weight of two people, while the other half tried to find a way of clinging on to the thick pipe, his last chance.

'Hold on to me,' he murmured.

Irene looked at him; then looked down at the ground.

'Oh my God!'

Ismael winked at her. 'Good luck,' he whispered.

The angel's claws sank into the stone only centimetres from Irene's face. She screamed, grabbed hold of Ismael, and closed her eyes. They were falling at dizzying speed. When she opened her eyes again, they seemed to be suspended in mid-air; Ismael was sliding down the pipe, barely able to control his fall. Irene's heart was in her mouth. Above them, the angel was hammering at the pipe, crushing it against the façade. Ismael could feel the skin on his hands and forearms burning. The angel started to climb down towards them but as it grasped the pipe, its weight wrenched the drain off the wall.

The creature's metallic frame plunged into the void, dragging the pipe with it, the whole thing arcing towards the ground with Ismael and Irene still attached. Ismael struggled not to lose his grip, but the pain and the speed with which they were falling were too much for him.

The pipe slipped out of his arms and the two found themselves falling towards the large pond that ran along the edge of the west wing of Cravenmoore. They hit the ice-cold surface of the water hard and sank towards the slimy bottom of the lake. Irene felt the water fill her nostrils and her burning throat. A wave of panic engulfed her. She opened her eyes but all she could see under the water was darkness. A shape appeared next to her: Ismael. The boy grabbed hold of her. Together, they rose to the surface and emerged, spluttering into the night air.

'Hurry,' Ismael urged her.

Irene noticed wounds on his hands and arms.

'It's nothing,' he lied, jumping out of the pond.

She followed him. The cold breeze glued her sodden clothes to her body, like a painful layer of frost touching her skin. Ismael scanned the shadows around them.

'Where is it?' asked Irene.

'Perhaps when it fell . . .'

Something moved in the bushes. Immediately they recognised two scarlet eyes. The angel was still there and it was not going to let them get away alive.

'Run!'

They dashed towards the entrance to the forest, their wet clothes slowing their progress and chilling them to the bone. They could hear the sound of the angel moving through the undergrowth. Clutching Irene's hand, Ismael headed for the deepest part of the wood, which was shrouded in fog.

'Where are we going?' Irene asked, aware that they were entering an unfamiliar part of the forest.

Ismael didn't bother to reply; he just kept pulling her forward, desperately. Irene could feel the bushes scraping the skin round her ankles and she was weak with exhaustion. She couldn't keep up this pace much longer. Soon the creature would catch up with them and tear them to pieces with its claws.

'I can't go on . . .'

'Yes, you can!'

Ismael's head was spinning and he could hear the branches breaking only a few metres behind them. For a moment he thought he was going to faint, but a sharp stab of pain in his leg revived him: one of the angel's claws had emerged from the bushes and slashed at his thigh. Irene screamed and tried to close her eyes, but she couldn't look away from the nightmarish face of their predator.

At that very moment they stumbled on the entrance to a cave, half concealed by the vegetation. Ismael threw himself inside, pulling Irene with him. So this was where he was taking her. A cave. Didn't Ismael think the angel would follow them inside? The only reply Irene heard was the sound of claws scratching against the rocky walls. Ismael dragged her along the narrow tunnel until they reached a hole in the ground, a vertical drop into a bottomless pit. A cold salty breeze rose from the void and from somewhere down below came a powerful rumbling sound. The sea.

'Jump!' Ismael ordered.

Irene stared at the black hole. A direct entrance into hell would have seemed more inviting.

'What's down there?'

Ismael sighed. The angel could be heard close behind them. Very close.

'It's an entrance to the Cave of Bats.'

'The second entrance? You said it was dangerous!'

'We have no choice . . .'

Their eyes met in the gloom. Two metres away, the dark angel appeared, flexing its claws. Ismael gave a nod. Irene took his hand and they jumped into the void. Hurling itself after them, the angel tumbled through the hole into the Cave of Bats.

To Ismael and Irene, the fall through the dark seemed endless, and when their bodies finally plunged into the sea, they felt the cold water biting into every pore. As they floated up to the surface, the tide propelled them towards the sharp rocky walls.

'Where is it?' asked Irene, struggling to control her shivering.

For a few seconds, they embraced without saying a word, expecting the hellish apparition to emerge from the sea at any moment and end their lives in the darkness of the cave. But that moment never came. Ismael was the first to notice.

The angel's scarlet eyes shone up from the depths; the creature's enormous weight prevented it from floating to the surface. A roar of anger reached them through the water. Whatever was manipulating the angel was twisting about furiously, conscious that its puppet had fallen into a trap that rendered it useless. The huge mass of metal would never reach the surface and was condemned to remain at the bottom of the cave until the sea turned it into a pile of rusty scrap.

The two friends remained there, watching the glow

of those eyes fade then disappear beneath the water for ever. Ismael let out a sigh of relief. Irene quietly wept.

'It's over,' she said in a shaky voice. 'It's over.'

'No,' replied Ismael. 'That was only a machine: it had no life or will of its own. Something was making it move and that something tried to kill us . . .'

'But what is it?'

'I don't know . . .'

As they spoke, there was a sudden explosion at the bottom of the cave. A cloud of black bubbles rose to the surface, then morphed into a dark spectre that scaled the rock towards the roof of the cave. The shadow stopped and observed them from its perch.

'Is it leaving?' whispered Irene, terror-stricken.

Cruel laughter filled the grotto. Ismael shook his head.

'It's leaving us here . . .' said the boy. 'The tide will do the rest . . .'

The shadow vanished through the entrance hole in the roof.

Ismael led Irene to a small rock that jutted out above the water's surface. There was just enough space for the two of them. He put his arms around her. They were wounded and shivering with cold, but for a few moments they just lay on the rock and took deep breaths, without saying a word. At some point, Ismael noticed that the sea seemed to be touching his feet again and realised that the tide was rising. It wasn't the creature pursuing them that had fallen into a trap, but themselves.

The shadow had abandoned them to the mercy of a slow and terrible death.

10. TRAPPED

The sea roared as it crashed against the mouth of the cave. The entrance hole above them was far away and unattainable, like the eye of a dome. In just a few minutes the sea level had already risen several centimetres. It wasn't long before Irene noticed that the area of the rock they were sitting on, like castaways, was getting smaller.

'The tide is rising,' she said in a hushed voice.

All Ismael could do was nod dejectedly.

'What will happen to us?' She had already guessed the answer, but was hoping that Ismael, who seemed to possess an endless supply of surprises, might have something else up his sleeve.

He turned his eyes towards her gloomily. Irene's hopes vanished in an instant.

'As the tide rises it blocks the main entrance to the cave,' Ismael explained. 'Then there's no other exit except through that hole in the ceiling.'

He paused and buried his head in his hands.

The thought of waiting until they slowly drowned like rats in the rising tide made Irene's blood run cold.

'There has to be some other way of getting out of

here,' she said.

'There isn't.'

'So what are we going to do?'

'For the moment, just wait . . .'

Irene realised that she couldn't keep expecting Ismael to come up with answers. He was probably even more frightened than she was, only too aware of the dangers of the cave. Come to think of it, changing the subject might not be a bad idea.

'There's something . . . While we were inside Cravenmoore,' she began hesitantly. 'When I went into that room, I saw something there. Something relating to Alma Maltisse . . .'

Ismael gave her a puzzled look.

'I think . . . I think Alma Maltisse and Alexandra Jann are one and the same person. Alma Maltisse was Alexandra's maiden name, before she married Lazarus,' Irene explained.

'That's impossible. Alma Maltisse drowned years ago,' Ismael objected.

'But nobody found her body . . .'

'It's impossible,' Ismael insisted.

'While I was in the room, I noticed her portrait and . . . there was somebody lying on the bed. A woman.'

Ismael rubbed his eyes, trying to put his thoughts in order.

'Just a moment. Supposing you're right. Suppose Alma Maltisse and Alexandra Jann are the same person. Then who is the woman you saw in Cravenmoore? Who is the woman who has been shut up there, all

150

these years, pretending to be Lazarus's sick wife?'

'I don't know . . . The more we find out, the less I understand what's going on,' said Irene. 'And there's something else that's worrying me. What was that figure we saw in the toy factory? It looked like my mother. Just thinking about it makes my hair stand on end. Lazarus is building an automaton with my mother's face . . .'

A surge of freezing water soaked their ankles. The sea level had risen at least twenty centimetres since they'd hauled themselves onto the rock. They exchanged a look of desperation. The sea roared again and a gush of water thundered through the entrance to the cave.

Midnight had left a wreath of fog over the cliffs that rose from the jetty to Seaview. The oil lamp was still swinging in the porch, its flame almost out. Apart from the rumour of the sea and the whisper of leaves in the forest, the silence was almost complete. Dorian was lying on his bed, holding a small glass with a lighted candle inside it. He didn't want his mother to see that his light was still on, and besides, he didn't trust the bedside lamp after what had happened before. The flame danced under his breath like some fiery spirit, revealing strange shapes and shadows in every corner. Dorian sighed. He wouldn't be able to sleep a wink that night, not for all the gold in the world.

Shortly after saying goodbye to Lazarus, Simone had put her head round his bedroom door to make sure

Dorian was all right. He had curled up under the sheets, fully dressed, pretending to sleep, and his mother had retired to her room to follow his example. That was hours ago now. In the seemingly endless wait for dawn to arrive, every glimmer of light, every creak, every shadow, threatened to set his heart racing.

Slowly, the flame died down until it was a tiny blue bubble, so faint it made barely any difference to the gloom. A moment later, darkness regained the room, little by little. Dorian could feel the drips of hot candle wax hardening in the glass. Only a few centimetres away, on the bedside table, the small angel Lazarus had given him was watching him in silence.

He threw the bedclothes aside and got up. He decided not to put on any shoes, to avoid the tumult of creaking his feet seemed to make whenever he tried to move about quietly in Seaview. Then, gathering all the courage he could muster, he tiptoed across his bedroom to the door. Turning the doorknob and opening the door without the usual concert of rusty hinges took him ten long seconds, but was worth it. Dorian closed the door behind him and crept to the top of the staircase, past the entrance to Irene's bedroom.

His sister had gone to bed hours ago, feigning a terrible headache, although Dorian suspected she was probably intending to read or write syrupy love letters to that sailor boyfriend of hers. She seemed to be spending more than twenty-four hours a day with him. Ever since he'd seen her wearing that dress of his mother's, he'd known there was trouble ahead.

When he reached the ground floor, Dorian noticed that the house was encircled by a ring of fog. Coils of mist seemed to slither over it, searching for a way in. 'Condensed water vapour,' he told himself. 'It's only condensed vapour moving about. Basic chemistry.' Having reassured himself with this scientific explanation, he ignored the wisps of fog filtering through the gaps in the windows and went into the kitchen. When he got there, he realised that the romance between Irene and Captain Fantastic had its positive side: since she'd started going out with him, his sister hadn't touched the delicious box of Swiss chocolates Simone kept on the second shelf of the food cupboard. Dorian remembered his mother once joking that chocolate had all of the chemical benefits of love and none of its noxious side effects.

Licking his lips, Dorian attacked the first chocolate. An exquisite burst of truffle, almonds and cocoa numbed his senses. This was what Greta Garbo's kisses must taste like. As far as he was concerned, after maps, chocolate was probably the finest invention the human race had come up with. Especially whole boxes of chocolates. 'Clever people, the Swiss,' thought Dorian. 'Clocks and chocolates: the essential things in life.' A sudden noise startled him away from such comforting thoughts. Dorian heard the noise again: paralysed with fear, he let the second chocolate slip through his fingers. Somebody was knocking on the door.

He tried to swallow, but his mouth was too dry. Two more sharp knocks. Dorian entered the living room, his eyes glued to the front door. Fog was seeping in under the door frame. Two more knocks. Dorian stopped, facing the door, hesitating for a moment.

'Who is it?' he asked, his voice faltering.

Two further knocks were his only reply. He went over to the window, but the blanket of fog blocked the view completely. He couldn't hear any footsteps on the porch. Perhaps the stranger had left. 'Probably someone who is lost,' thought Dorian. He was about to return to the kitchen when the two knocks came again, but this time they were on the windowpane, ten centimetres away from his face. His heart skipped a beat. Slowly, Dorian walked backwards, moving into the centre of the living room until he bumped into a chair. Instinctively, he grabbed hold of a metal candlestick and brandished it in front him.

'Go away,' he whispered.

For a split second, a face seemed to form in the mist on the other side of the glass. Moments later, the window was flung open by a gale-force wind that sent icy shock waves through Dorian's body. Horrified, he watched as a black stain spread across the floor.

A shadow.

The shape halted in front of him and slowly coalesced, rising from the floor like a puppet pulled by invisible strings. The boy tried to hit the intruder with the candlestick, but the metal passed straight through it. Dorian took another step back as the shadow floated towards him. Two misty black hands gripped his throat; he felt their icy touch on his skin. A face appeared.

Dorian shivered from head to toe when he saw his father's features materialise only centimetres from his face. Armand Sauvelle smiled but it was a cruel smile, full of hatred.

'Hello, Dorian,' the shadow whispered. 'I've come to fetch your mother. Will you take me to her?'

The sound of the voice froze Dorian's soul. It was not his father's voice. Those demonic eyes were not his father's eyes. And those long, pointed teeth were not those of Armand Sauvelle.

'You're not my father . . .'

The wolfish smile vanished and the features melted away. A furious cry, like the howl of an animal, pierced Dorian's ears and an invisible force hurled him to the other side of the room. Dorian crashed into one of the armchairs, knocking it over.

Still dazed, the boy managed to get to his feet again, just in time to see the shadow sliding up the stairs like a moving pool of tar.

'Mother!' Dorian shouted, rushing towards the staircase.

The shadow paused for a moment and fixed Dorian with its stare. Shiny black lips formed a soundless word. His name. Suddenly all the windowpanes in the house shattered and the fog engulfed Seaview with a roar as the shadow continued its ascent to the next floor. Dorian rushed after it, pursuing the ghostly shape as it advanced towards his mother's bedroom.

'No!' he yelled. 'Don't you touch my mother.'

The shadow grinned at him and a moment later the

black mass turned into a whirlwind that spun through the bedroom keyhole. A deathly silence followed.

Dorian ran towards the door, but before he could reach it, the wooden panel burst outward with such force that the door was yanked off its hinges and dashed against the opposite wall. Dorian threw himself to one side, managing to dodge it by just a few millimetres.

When he got to his feet again, the scene that met his eyes was like something out of a nightmare. The shadow was crawling along the walls of his mother's room while she lay unconscious on her bed, her own shadow projected onto the wall. Dorian watched the black figure creep up to her shadow and brush the shape of her lips with its own. Simone stirred in her sleep, as if trapped in a bad dream. Two invisible hands seized her and lifted her from the sheets. Dorian stood in the way. Once more, an invisible force struck him and sent him flying out of the room. Carrying Simone in its arms, the shadow rushed down the stairs. Dorian stood up again, trying hard not to faint, and followed it to the ground floor. The spectre turned around and, for a moment, they stared at one another.

'I know who you are . . .' whispered the boy.

A new face, unfamiliar to him, made its appearance: the features were those of a handsome young man with luminous eyes.

'You don't know anything,' hissed the shadow.

Dorian noticed the spectre's eyes sweeping the room then pausing at the old wooden door that lead to the cellar. All of a sudden, the door burst open and the boy felt a powerful energy propelling him towards it. He tumbled down the dark staircase. Then the door slammed shut, booming like a slab of stone.

The last he heard before he lost consciousness was the shadow's howling laughter as it carried his mother towards the wood.

As the tide advanced inside the cave, Irene and Ismael felt the deathly trap tightening around them. Irene had already forgotten the moment when the water swamped their temporary refuge on the rock. Now there was nowhere left for them to stand and they were at the mercy of the sea. The cold tore at their muscles, like the pricking of hundreds of tiny pins, and they were losing all sensation in their hands. Exhaustion tugged at their legs, pulling them down. A voice inside them told them to let go, to surrender to the peaceful sleep that awaited them beneath the water. Ismael helped Irene to stay afloat. He could feel her body shivering in his arms. How long he'd be able to hang on, he didn't know. How long it would take for dawn to break and the water level to start going down, he knew even less.

'Don't let your arms drop. Move about. Keep moving,' he groaned.

Irene nodded.

'I'm sleepy . . .' she mumbled. She was almost delirious with exhaustion.

'No. You can't fall asleep now,' Ismael ordered her.

Irene gazed at him, her eyes half open. Ismael reached up and touched the rocky ceiling towards which the tide was carrying them. The current was moving them away from the hole in the roof, sending them into the very bowels of the cave and far from the only possible escape route. Despite all their efforts to remain beneath the entrance hole, there was no way they could keep themselves afloat and fight the unstoppable force of the current. There was barely enough room for them to breathe. And the tide kept rising.

For a moment, Irene's face dropped into the water. Ismael grabbed her and pulled her head out. The girl was in a complete daze. He knew of stronger and much more experienced seamen who had died in this way, abandoned to their fate in the ocean. The cold could do this to anyone. First it numbed your muscles and dulled your mind, then it waited patiently for you to fall into its arms and pulled you under a shroud of cold and darkness.

Ismael shook Irene and turned her towards him. She mumbled something unintelligible. Without flinching, Ismael slapped her hard. Irene opened her eyes and screamed. For a few seconds she didn't know where she was. In the dark, surrounded by icy water, with some stranger's arms around her; she thought she was in the middle of her worst nightmare. Then, everything came back to her. Cravenmoore. The angel. The cave. As Ismael hugged her she could not stop her tears and she whimpered like a frightened child.

'Don't let me die here,' she whispered.

'You're not going to die here. I promise. I won't

allow it. The tide will soon start to ebb and perhaps the cave won't fill up completely . . . We must hang on a little longer. Only a little while and then we'll be able to get out of here.'

Irene nodded and hugged him even tighter. If only Ismael could believe his words as much as she did.

Lazarus Jann slowly climbed Cravenmoore's main staircase. A presence floated in the halo projected by the glass turret. He could sense it, smell it in the air, in the way the specks of dust seemed to mesh together in the light. When he reached the second floor his eyes rested on the door at the end of the corridor. It was open. His hands began to shake.

'Alexandra?'

The cold breath of the wind lifted the gauze curtain hanging in the corridor. A dark foreboding came over him. Lazarus closed his eyes and put his hand to his side. A sharp pain which had started in his chest was spreading like wildfire down his right arm.

'Alexandra?' he cried again.

Lazarus ran to the bedroom door but stopped when he saw the signs of the struggle and the cold mist drifting in from the forest through the broken windows. He clenched his fists until he felt his nails digging into his palms.

'Damn you . . .'

Mopping the cold sweat from his forehead, he walked over to the bed and with infinite care pulled aside the curtains.

'I'm sorry, dearest . . .' he said, sitting on the edge of the bed. 'I'm sorry . . .'

A strange sound caught his attention. The bedroom door was swinging from side to side. Lazarus stood up and cautiously walked towards it.

'Who's there?' he said.

There was no reply, but the door stopped moving. Lazarus took a few steps into the corridor and scanned the darkness. By the time he heard the hissing above him it was too late. A sharp blow to the back of his neck knocked him down, rendering him half unconscious. He could feel a pair of hands grabbing him by the shoulders and dragging him down the passage. He managed to get a glimpse of what was happening: Christian, the automaton he kept by the main door. The face turned towards him. A cruel glow lit up its eyes.

Moments later, Lazarus lost consciousness altogether.

Ismael sensed the arrival of dawn when the currents that had been pushing them towards the deepest part of the cave began to recede. The ocean's invisible hands decided to let go of their prey, allowing him to drag Irene towards the highest point of the ceiling, where the water level afforded them a larger pocket of air. When the first shaft of daylight glinted on the sandy seabed, tracing a path towards the exit of the cave, Ismael let out a scream of joy that nobody, not even his friend, could hear. The boy knew that once the sea level began to fall, the cave would reveal the way out to the lagoon and the open air.

For the last couple of hours Irene had only kept afloat with Ismael's help. She could barely stay awake and her body swayed in the current like a lifeless object. While he waited for the tide to allow them a passageway out of there, Ismael realised that, had he not been there, Irene would have died hours ago.

As he whispered words of encouragement she could not understand, Ismael recalled tales he'd heard from old sailors about their encounters with death. They said that when a person saved another at sea their souls were for ever tied by an invisible thread.

Bit by bit, the current ebbed and Ismael managed to drag Irene towards the lagoon, leaving the mouth of the cave behind them. As the first light of day spilled over the horizon, the boy guided Irene to the shore. When she opened her eyes, she saw Ismael's smiling face gazing down at her.

'We're alive,' he said.

Irene let her eyelids drop in exhaustion.

Ismael took one last look at the colours of dawn illuminating the forest and the cliffs. It was the most marvellous sight he had ever witnessed. Then he lay down on the white sand and yielded to sleep. Nothing could have roused them from that slumber. Nothing.

11. THE FACE BENEATH THE MASK

The first thing Irene saw when she awoke was a pair of black eyes calmly observing her. She jerked backwards and the frightened seagull flew off. Her lips felt dry and sore, her skin so tight it ached. Her muscles were as limp as rags and her brain pure jelly. She felt a wave of nausea rising from the pit of her stomach. When she tried to sit up, she realised that the strange fire gnawing at her skin was in fact the sun. There was a bitter taste on her lips. What seemed to be a small beach surrounded by rocks floated about her like a merry-go-round. She had never felt so ill in her life.

She lay down again and became aware of Ismael's presence next to her. If it hadn't been for his fitful breathing, Irene would have sworn he was dead. She rubbed her eyes and placed one of her hands on his neck. A pulse. Irene stroked Ismael's face and after a while he opened his eyes. The sun blinded him for a moment.

'You look dreadful . . .' he mumbled, trying to smile.

'You haven't seen yourself,' replied Irene.

Like two castaways swept ashore by a storm, they

stumbled to their feet and searched for shade to protect them. They found it beneath the remains of a tree trunk that had fallen among the rocks. The seagull that had been watching them sleep alighted on the sand again, still curious.

'What time could it be?' asked Irene, fighting the hammering in her temples that accompanied every word.

Ismael showed her his watch. The face was full of water, and the second hand, which had come loose, looked like a petrified eel. He shaded his eyes with both hands and looked up at the sun.

'It's after midday.'

'How long have we been asleep?'

'Not long enough,' replied Ismael. 'I could sleep for a week.'

'We can't sleep now,' Irene urged him.

He nodded and scanned the cliffs for a possible way out.

'It won't be easy. I only know how to get to the lagoon by sea . . .'

'What is behind the cliffs?

'The forest we went through yesterday.'

'So what are we waiting for?'

Ismael examined the jumble of sharp rocks that rose before them. To scale the cliffs would take some time, and considerable effort. The image of an egg cracking open as it hit the ground ran through his mind. 'A perfect ending,' he thought.

'Can you climb?' asked Ismael.

Irene shrugged. He noticed her bare feet, covered in sand. Pale-skinned arms and legs, totally unprotected.

'I used to do gym at school and I was one of the best at climbing up a rope,' she added. 'I suppose it's the same thing.'

Ismael sighed. Their problems were certainly not at an end.

For a few moments Simone Sauvelle was eight years old again. Again she smelled the intense aroma of molten wax, heard voices whispering in the dark, saw the dance of hundreds of burning candles. She was back in that enchanted place that had captivated her as a child: the old cathedral of Saint-Etienne. But the magic only lasted a few seconds.

Then, as her tired eyes became accustomed to the thick darkness surrounding her, Simone realised that the candles didn't belong to any chapel, that the patches of light dancing on the walls were old photographs and that the voices, those distant echoes, existed only in her mind. She knew instinctively that she wasn't in Seaview, or in any other place she could remember. Her memory produced a confused echo of the last hours. She remembered having spoken to Lazarus on the porch. She remembered having made herself a glass of hot milk before going to bed, and she remembered the last words she'd read in the book that lay on her bedside table.

After turning off the light, she vaguely recalled having dreamed about a boy screaming. She also had the absurd feeling that she'd woken up in the middle of the night to see shadows walking through the darkness. Other than that, nothing: her memory came to an end, like the edges of an unfinished drawing. Her hands felt the touch of cotton and she realised that she was still wearing her nightdress. She stood up and walked over to a mural that was lit by dozens of white candles, all neatly aligned on candelabra, each heavy with tears of wax.

The flames seemed to whisper in unison; these were the voices she thought she'd heard. Her eyes widened in the golden glow and a strange lucidity filled her mind. More memories seemed to return, one by one, like the first drops of rain. With them came the first wave of panic.

She remembered the cold feeling of invisible hands dragging her through the dark. She remembered a voice murmuring in her ear as every muscle in her body turned to stone. She remembered a shape forged of shadows hauling her through the forest. She remembered how it had whispered her name and how, terror-stricken, she had realised that none of this was a nightmare. Simone closed her eyes and clasped her hand over her mouth to stop herself from screaming.

Her first thought was for her children. What had happened to Dorian and Irene? Were they still in the house? Had that unspeakable apparition caught them? Each question seared her soul. She ran towards what looked like a door and hammered at it, screaming and crying until she was overcome with exhaustion. Slowly, an icy calmness brought her back to reality.

She was trapped. Whoever had kidnapped her and locked her up had probably also captured her children. The thought that they could be hurt or wounded was something she could not contemplate. If she hoped to do anything for them, she must not panic. Simone clenched her fists tightly and repeated those words in her mind. She took a deep breath and looked carefully around the room. The sooner she understood what was going on, the sooner she'd be able to get out of there and go in search of Irene and Dorian.

The first thing her eyes registered were pieces of furniture, small and simply made: children's furniture. She was in a child's room, but she knew instinctively that no child had lived there for a long time. The presence pervading that place radiated an aura of old age and decay. Simone moved over to the bed and sat on it, gazing at the room. There was no innocence in that bedroom. All she could sense was darkness. Evil.

The slow poison of fear began to course through her veins, but Simone ignored the warning. Instead she picked up one of the candlesticks and returned to the mural. It was composed of endless newspaper cuttings and photographs. She noticed the unusual neatness with which the images had been stuck to the wall. She brought the candle closer and let the torrent of photographs, prints, words and drawings invade her mind.

Suddenly she came across a familiar name: Daniel Hoffmann. The mysterious character from Berlin whose letters she was instructed to set aside and whose correspondence, as Simone had accidentally discovered, ended up in the fire. She started reading. Something about the whole business didn't add up. The man referred to in the news articles didn't live in Berlin and, judging from the date the newspapers were published, he would by now have reached an improbable old age. Bewildered, Simone read on.

This Hoffmann was a wealthy man – a fantastically wealthy man. Slightly further along, the front page of *Le Figaro* detailed the news about a fire in a toy factory. A person called Daniel Hoffmann had perished in the flames. The image accompanying the article showed the blaze destroying the building as a crowd looked on. Among them was a boy who seemed lost, staring at the camera with frightened eyes.

The same face appeared in another clipping. This time the item told the disturbing story of a boy who had spent seven days locked in a dark cellar. Police officers had found him after discovering his dead mother in another room. The boy's expression — he couldn't have been more than seven or eight – seemed vacant, unfathomable.

She shuddered as the pieces of the jigsaw began to come together in her mind. But there was more. The cuttings advanced through time. Many of them referred to people who had disappeared, people Simone had never heard of. Among them an extraordinarily beautiful young woman called Alexandra Alma Maltisse, heiress to a metal-forging business in Lyon. A magazine published in Marseille referred to her as the fiancée of a young but already renowned engineer, Lazarus Jann. Next to that cutting was a series of photographs showing the handsome couple donating toys to an orphanage in Le Marais. They both glowed with happiness. 'I'm determined to ensure that every child in this country, whatever their situation, has a toy to play with,' the inventor declared in the caption.

Further on, another article announced the wedding of Lazarus Jann and Alexandra Maltisse. The official engagement photograph had been taken at the foot of the stairway leading up to Cravenmoore. In the image, a very youthful Lazarus embraced his fiancée. It all seemed like a daydream staged for the glossy magazines. The young, enterprising Jann had acquired the sumptuous mansion with the idea of making it their marital home. Various images of Cravenmoore illustrated the item.

The succession of cuttings and photographs went on and on, ushering in characters and events from the past. Simone paused and went back to the beginning. The face of the terrified boy wouldn't let go of her. She gazed into those lonely eyes and gradually began to recognise the features on which she had pinned all her hopes and to which she had pledged her friendship. That tortured gaze did not belong to Jean Neville, the boy in Lazarus's story. It was a face she knew well, painfully well. It was the face of Lazarus Jann.

A dark cloud settled on her heart. She took a deep breath and closed her eyes. For some reason, even before the voice spoke, Simone knew there was someone else in the room.

Irene and Ismael reached the clifftop shortly before four o'clock. The climb had left a trail of bruises and cuts on their arms and legs. However hard Ismael had predicted it would be, the ascent turned out to be far worse and much more dangerous than he could have anticipated. Irene, who hadn't said a word or opened her mouth to complain about her painful wounds, had shown a courage he'd never witnessed before. She had ventured up crags nobody in their right mind would have attempted. When at last they reached the entrance to the wood, Ismael could only hug her.

'Tired?'

Breathless, Irene shook her head.

'Has anyone ever told you you're the most stubborn person on the planet?'

A smile appeared on her lips.

'Wait till you meet my mother.'

Before Ismael could reply, she took his hand and pulled him towards the wood.

Simone slowly turned round to face the shadows. She could feel the presence of the intruder; she could even hear the muffled sound of his breathing. But she couldn't see him. Simone scanned the darkness searching for the visitor. She felt an unexpected sense of calm, which allowed her to think clearly. Her senses were alert to every tiny detail, her mind registering every vibration of the air, every sound, every reflection with spine-chilling precision. Wrapped in this strange serenity, she stood in silence, waiting for the visitor to make himself known.

'I didn't expect to see you here,' said the voice at last, speaking from the shadows. 'Are you afraid?'

Simone shook her head.

'Good. You shouldn't be afraid.'

'Are you going to stay there, hiding, Lazarus?'

A long silence ensued. Lazarus's breathing became more audible.

'I'd rather stay here,' he replied at last.

'Why?'

Something glistened in the dark. A fleeting sparkle, almost imperceptible.

'Why don't you sit down, Madame Sauvelle?'

'I'd rather stand.'

'As you wish.' He paused again. 'You might be wondering what is going on.'

'Among other things,' interrupted Simone, unable to hide her indignation.

'Perhaps the easiest thing would be for you to ask the questions and I'll try to answer them.'

Simone sighed angrily. 'My first and last question is this: how do I get out of here?'

'I'm afraid that's not possible. Not yet.'

'Why not?'

'Is that another of your questions?'

'Where am I?'

'In Cravenmoore.'

'How did I get here?'

'Someone brought you . . .'

'You?'

'No.'

'Who?'

'Someone you don't know . . . yet.'

'Where are my children?'

'I don't know.'

Simone took a step into the shadows, her face flushed with anger.

'You bastard!'

She walked in the direction of the voice. Gradually, her eyes made out the outline of a person sitting in an armchair. Lazarus. But there was something odd about his face. Simone stopped.

'It's a mask,' he said.

'Why?' she asked. The calm she had experienced earlier was rapidly abandoning her.

'Masks reveal a person's true face . . .'

Simone struggled to maintain her composure. Getting angry wouldn't help her.

'Where are my children? Please . . .'

'I've already told you, Madame Sauvelle. I don't know.'

'What are you going to do with me?'

Lazarus unfolded one of his hands, encased in a satin glove. A glimmer of light caught the surface of the mask. That was the sparkle she'd noticed earlier.

'I'm not going to hurt you, Simone. You mustn't be afraid of me. You have to trust me.'

'That seems a little out of place, don't you think?'

'It's for your own good. I'm trying to protect you.'

'Who from?'

'Please sit down.'

'What on earth is going on here? Why won't you tell me?'

Simone noticed her voice becoming weak and childish. Realising she was close to hysteria, she clenched her fists and took a deep breath. She retreated a few steps and then sat on one of the chairs set around an empty table.

'Thank you,' murmured Lazarus.

A silent tear ran down her face.

'Before I say anything else, I want you to know that I'm truly sorry you've become mixed up in all this,' declared the toymaker. 'I never thought it would come to this.'

'There never was a boy called Jean Neville, was there?' asked Simone. 'That boy was you. The story you told me . . . was a half-truth derived from your own life.'

'I see you've been reading my collection of newspaper cuttings. That may have led you to form some interesting, but mistaken ideas.'

'The only idea I have formed, Mr Jann, is that you're sick and you need help. I don't know how you managed to drag me here, but I can assure you that as soon as I get out of this place, my first visit will be to the police station. Kidnapping is a crime . . .'

Her words sounded ridiculous in the context.

'May I infer that you're thinking of giving up your job, Madame Sauvelle?'

This strange piece of irony set alarm bells ringing. The Lazarus she knew would never make such a comment. Although, quite frankly, the only thing she was clear about was that she didn't know him at all.

'You can infer whatever you please,' she replied coldly.

'Good. In that case, before you go to the authorities, and you have my permission, let me complete the story that I'm sure you've already tried to piece together in your mind.'

Simone stared at the mask. It was pale and completely expressionless. A porcelain face. His eyes were two pools of darkness.

'As you will see, dear Simone, the only moral of this tale, or of any other, is that in real life, as opposed to fiction, nothing is what it seems . . .'

'Promise me one thing, Lazarus.'

'If it's in my power to do so . . .'

'Promise me that, if I listen to your story, you'll let me leave this place with my children. I swear I won't go to the authorities. I'll just take my family and abandon the village for ever. You'll never hear from me again.'

The mask was silent for a few seconds.

'Is that what you want?'

Simone nodded, holding back her tears.

'You disappoint me, Simone, I thought we were friends. Good friends.'

'Please . . .'

The masked man clenched his fists.

'All right. If you want to be reunited with your children, you shall be. In due course . . .'

'Do you remember your mother, Madame Sauvelle? Children always keep a special place in their hearts for the woman who gave life to them, or so the fairy tales would have us believe. It's like a spark of light that never goes out, they say. I do believe that. In fact, I've spent most of my life trying to put out that light. But it's not easy. And I hope that, before you condemn me, you'll be kind enough to hear me out. I'll be brief.

'I was born in Paris on the night of 26 December 1882, in an old house on one of the most miserable streets in the Gobelins. A gloomy, unhealthy place to live if ever there was one. That is where my mother, with the help of her neighbour Nicole, gave birth to a little baby. It was such a cold winter that apparently a few minutes went by before I started to cry the way all babies do. So, for a moment, my mother was convinced that I had been stillborn. When she realised that it was not so, the poor wretch took this to be a miracle and decided – she regarded herself as devout to the point of holiness – to christen me Lazarus.

'I recall the years of my childhood as a succession of endless fighting in the streets and my mother's long illnesses. One of my earliest memories is sitting on Nicole's knees and listening to the kind woman tell me that my mother was very ill, that she could not respond to my cries and that I must be a good boy and go and play with the other children. The other children she was referring to were a group of ragged kids who went around stealing from dawn to dusk and who, by the age of seven, had learned that in our district survival meant becoming either a criminal or a civil servant. I don't need to tell you which of the alternatives they favoured.

'In those days, the only glimmer of hope was provided by a mysterious character who haunted our dreams. To us, his name, Daniel Hoffmann, was synonymous with our fantasies – so much so that many of the children doubted his existence. Legend had it that Hoffmann wandered through the streets of Paris, wearing different disguises, assuming different identities, and providing poor children with toys which he had made in his factory. Every child in Paris had heard of him and they all dreamed that one day they would be the lucky one.

'Hoffmann was a master of magic and imagination. Only one thing could overcome his power to intrigue: age. As children grew older and their spirit lost its ability to imagine and invent, the name of Daniel Hoffmann eventually faded from their minds; until one day, when they were adults, it no longer meant a thing to them, even when they heard the name uttered by their own children . . .

'Daniel Hoffmann was the greatest toy manufacturer that ever lived. He owned a large factory in Les Gobelins. It was like an enormous cathedral rising from the squalor of that ghostly quarter. From its centre soared a tower, sharp as a needle, piercing the clouds. Its bells marked dawn and dusk every day, and the echo of those bells could be heard all over Paris, beckoning. All the children in the city knew that building, but the truly amazing thing was that adults were incapable of seeing it. Age had blinded them and they were convinced that the site was occupied by a vast swamp, a wasteland at the heart of the poorest area of Paris.

'Nobody had ever set eyes on the real Daniel Hoffmann. People said that the toymaker lived in a room at the top of the tower and hardly ever left it, except when he ventured out into the streets at nightfall, in disguise, handing out toys to the city's dispossessed. In exchange he asked for one thing only: the children's hearts, their promise of eternal love and obedience. In our area, any child would have surrendered his heart without giving it a second thought. But not every child heard the call. Rumour had it that he used hundreds of different disguises to conceal his identity. Some even swore that Daniel Hoffmann never wore the same outfit twice. He was everywhere and nowhere. A watcher in the shadows.

'But let's get back to my mother. The illness Nicole was referring to is still a mystery to me. I imagine that some people, like some toys, are born defective – which I suppose makes us all broken toys, don't you think? The truth is that, as time went by, my mother's illness led to her gradually losing her mental faculties, which, to be honest, had never really amounted to much to begin with. But when the body is wounded, it doesn't take long for the mind to follow suit.

'That is how I learned to grow up with loneliness as my only companion, dreaming that one day Daniel Hoffmann would come to my rescue. I remember that every night, before going to bed, I would ask my guardian angel to take me to him. Every night. And that is also how, probably inspired by the legend, I started to build my own toys.

'I used scraps I found in rubbish dumps across the district. I built my own train, and a three-storey castle. This was followed by a cardboard dragon and, later, a flying machine, long before aeroplanes had become a common sight in the skies. But my favourite toy was Gabriel. Gabriel was an angel. A wondrous angel I built with my own hands to protect me from the dark and the dangers fate might throw at me. I built it using the wreckage of an ironing machine and other pieces of scrap I found in an abandoned textile mill two blocks away from where we lived. But the life of Gabriel, my guardian angel, was short.

'The day my mother discovered my collection of toys was a death sentence for Gabriel. She dragged me down to the cellar of our building. She started muttering, looking around her as if there might be something lurking in the shadows, and told me that someone had been whispering to her in her dreams. My dear mother was one of those people who would never listen to anybody around her, but heard plenty of voices inside her head. One of those voices had informed her that toys – all toys – were the invention of Lucifer himself. She was always one to see the devil in the details – especially in other people. In her new-found wisdom she had decided that through toys the devil planned to steal the souls of every child in the world. That very night, Gabriel and all my other toys ended up in the building's furnace.

'My mother insisted that we should destroy them together, make sure they turned to ashes and thus I could return to the path of righteousness. Otherwise, the shadow of my accursed soul would come and get me. Every lapse in my behaviour, every error, every disobedient act, would leave a mark on my shadow. She told me that my shadow was a reflection of how wicked and inconsiderate I was, and that it followed me wherever I went. I was only seven at the time. Sometimes I wished that her threat would come true and I would embrace that shadow. At least that way I'd be free of her.'

'You're insane . . .' whispered Simone.

The man in the mask laughed.

'Wait. It gets better. Soon after this baptism of fire, my dear mother's illness took a turn for the worse. She would shut me up in the basement because she said the shadow wouldn't be able to find me there. At first, during these long spells I hardly dared breathe, fearing the sound of my breath might draw the shadow's attention and that this evil reflection of my corrupt soul would then carry me straight to hell. I realise all this must sound quite comical to you, or perhaps just sad, Madame Sauvelle, but for that young child it was a serious business indeed.

'I don't want to bore you with the sordid details. I'll just add that, during one of these purifying episodes, my mother finally lost what few, if any, marbles she had left and I ended up being trapped for a whole week in the darkness. You've already read the story in the cutting, I imagine: it was the kind of thing the press love to splash across their front pages. Bad news, especially if it's full of lurid details, is wonderful at persuading people to part with their money and remind them of how good they are, for evil is always on the other side of the fence, isn't it? You'll be wondering what a child does when he's locked up for seven days and seven nights in a dark basement waiting for the devil to come and claim his soul.

'First of all, you must understand that when humans are deprived of light, we lose all sense of time after a while. Hours turn into minutes or seconds, even weeks. Our perception of time is closely related to light. During that week something truly astonishing happened to me. A miracle. My second miracle, if you like, after those blank minutes that occurred after my birth.

'My prayers were answered. All those nights praying in silence had not been in vain. Call it luck, or fate, but Daniel Hoffmann finally came to me. To *me*. Of all the children in Paris, I was the chosen one. I still remember the timid rapping on the trapdoor that led to the street. I couldn't reach it, but I was able to reply to the voice that spoke to me from outside; the most marvellous, kindest voice I had ever heard. A voice that dispelled the darkness and melted away the fear of a frightened little boy, like sun melting ice. And do you know something? Daniel Hoffmann called me by my name.

'I opened the door of my heart to him. Suddenly, a wonderful light flooded the basement and Hoffmann appeared out of nowhere, dressed in a dazzling white suit. If only you'd seen him, Simone. He was an angel, a real angel of light. I've never seen anyone radiate such an aura of beauty and peace.

'That night, Daniel Hoffmann and I spoke in private, just as you and I are doing now. I didn't need to tell him about Gabriel and the rest of my toys; he already knew. He was also aware of the stories my mother had told me about the shadow. It was a relief to confess to him how terrified I was of it. He listened patiently as I recounted all the things that had happened to me, and I could feel he shared my pain and anxiety. His compassion and understanding were overwhelming. Above all, he understood that this shadow was my greatest fear, my worst nightmare. My own shadow, that evil spirit that followed me everywhere, the vessel for all the wickedness that was inside me . . .

'It was Daniel Hoffmann who told me what I had to do. Needless to say, I was completely ignorant at the time. What did I know about shadows? What did I know about mysterious spirits that visited people in their dreams and spoke to them about the future and the past? Nothing.

'But he did know. He knew *everything*. And he was willing to help me.

'That night, Daniel Hoffmann revealed my future to me. He told me that I was destined to succeed him as the head of his empire. He explained that all of his knowledge and his skill would one day be mine, and that the poverty that surrounded me would be gone for ever. He offered me prospects, things I could never have dreamed of. In short, he offered me a future. I had to do only one thing in exchange. A small, insignificant promise: I had to give him my heart. Give my heart to him and nobody else.

'The toymaker asked me whether I understood what that meant. I replied that I did, without a moment's hesitation. Of course he could have my heart. He was the only one who had ever been good to me. The only one to whom I mattered. He told me that, if I wished, he could get me out of there and I'd never have to see that house or that street, and especially my mother, again. Most importantly, he told me to stop worrying about the shadow. If I did what he asked of me, the future would open up to me; it would be bright, luminous.

'He wanted to know whether I trusted him. I said of course I did. He then took out a small glass bottle, the type of flask you'd use for perfume. He opened it with a smile and what happened next was truly amazing. The best trick I've ever seen. My shadow, my reflection on the wall, was transformed into a cloud of darkness that was consumed by the bottle, captured for ever inside it. Daniel Hoffmann closed the bottle and gave it to me. The glass felt icy cold against my skin.

'Hoffmann then explained that, from that moment on, my heart belonged to him and soon, very soon, all my problems would disappear – as long as I didn't go back on my word. I told him I'd never do such a thing. He asked me to close my eyes and think about what I most wished for in the entire universe. While I was doing that, he knelt down in front of me and kissed my forehead. When I opened my eyes he was gone.

'One week after my mother had locked me up, the police, alerted by someone who told them what was going on in my home, rescued me from that hole. My mother was found dead upstairs.

'On the way to the police station, the streets were filled with fire engines. You could smell the acrid smoke in the air. Ashes were raining from gray, steely skies. The policemen who were escorting me took a detour and that was when I saw it: towering in the distance, Daniel Hoffmann's factory was ablaze. It was the most terrible fire ever witnessed in Paris. Crowds who had been oblivious to it before now watched as the immense building burned to the ground. Suddenly everyone remembered the name of the character who had filled their childhood with dreams: Daniel Hoffmann. The watcher in the shadows had set his palace aflame. It was beautiful. Beautiful . . .

'Flames and plumes of black smoke rose heavenward for three days and three nights, as if hell itself had opened its doors to the city. I was there and I saw it with my own eyes. A few days later, when all that was left of the building was a pile of smoking rubble, the newspapers published the story. You know the press, they always get it late and wrong – that is, when they don't just go ahead and lie.

'In time, the authorities located one of my mother's relatives,who became my guardian. I moved to the south, to Antibes, to live with his family. I was raised and educated there, a normal life. Happy. Just as Daniel Hoffmann had promised. I even invented a different past for myself: the story I told you.

'The day I turned eighteen I received a letter. The Paris postmark was dated eight years earlier. In the letter, my old friend informed me that the law firm of a certain Monsieur Gilbert Travant, in the rue de Rivoli, held the title deeds to a residence on the coast of Normandy which would legally become mine when I came of age. The note, written on parchment, was signed with a D.

'A few years passed before I took possession of Cravenmoore. By then I was a promising engineer and my designs for toys surpassed anything known to man or child. I soon realised that it was time for me to set up my own factory. At Cravenmoore. Everything was unfolding just as I had been told. Everything, until the "accident" occurred. It happened on 13 February in the rue Soufflot, as I was walking out of the Pantheon. Her name was Alexandra Alma Maltisse and she was the most beautiful creature I had ever seen.

'All those years I'd kept the flask Daniel Hoffmann had given me that night, sequestered in a solid-steel box with a lock the combination of which only I knew. It remained as cold to the touch as it had always been. Colder than ice. So cold it cut your skin like the sharpest razor if you held it in your hand. But six months later, I forgot the promise I had made to him and gave my heart to that young woman. I was young and foolish and thought my life belonged to me, as all young and foolish people do. I married her and it was the happiest day of my life. The night before the wedding, which was to take place in Cravenmoore, I took the bottle containing my shadow, walked to the cliffs, and threw the bottle into the dark waters, sending it to oblivion.

'A word of advice, Madame Sauvelle: never make promises you're bound to break.'

The sun had begun its descent into the bay when Ismael and Irene glimpsed the rear wall of Seaview through the trees. Their exhaustion seemed to have retreated, as if waiting for a better moment to come back with a vengeance.

'What are you thinking about?' asked Irene, noticing Ismael's pensive expression.

'I'm thinking about how hungry I am.'

'Me too.'

'There's nothing like a good fright to give you an appetite,' Ismael joked.

Seaview was quiet. There didn't appear to be

anyone around. Two garlands of washing flapped on the clothes line. Ismael caught a fleeting glimpse of what looked like underwear. He stopped to consider what Irene might look like wearing it.

'Are you all right?' she asked.

The boy coughed.

'Tired and hungry, that's all.'

Irene tried to open the back door, but it appeared to be locked from the inside. She looked puzzled.

'Mum? Dorian?' she called. She took a few steps back and looked up at the windows on the first floor.

'Let's try the front,' said Ismael.

She followed him round the house to the porch, where they found a carpet of broken glass. They both stood in shocked silence at the sight that met their eyes: the door destroyed and the windows smashed to smithereens. At first glance it looked as if there might have been a gas explosion, tearing the door off its hinges. Irene tried to stop the wave of nausea rising from the pit of her stomach. Terrified, she gave Ismael a look then started walking towards the front door. He stopped her.

'Madame Sauvelle?' he called out from the porch.

The sound of his voice was lost inside the house. Cautiously Ismael entered the building and examined the scene, Irene peering anxiously over his shoulder.

What greeted them was nothing short of devastation. Ismael had never seen the effects of a tornado, but he imagined they must be something like this.

'My God . . .'

'Mind the glass,' Ismael warned Irene.

'Mum!'

Her shout echoed through the house, like a spirit wandering from room to room. Without letting go of Irene's hand, Ismael moved to the foot of the stairs.

'We have to go up,' she said.

They climbed the stairs, examining the trail that some invisible force had left behind. The first to notice that Simone's room no longer had a door was Irene.

'No!'

Ismael hurried over to the threshold and looked in. Nothing. One by one, they searched all the rooms on the first floor. All empty.

'Where are they?' asked Irene, her voice shaking.

'There's nobody here. Let's go downstairs.'

From what they could see, the fight or whatever it was that had taken place there, had been brutal. Ismael made no comment, but a dark suspicion concerning the fate of Irene's family crossed his mind. Irene wept quietly at the foot of the stairs, still in shock. His mind was racing through their options, each more useless than the last, when they both heard someone knocking.

Irene looked up, tearful. Ismael nodded, lifting a finger to his lips. The knocks were repeated; dry with a metallic ring, they seemed to travel through the structure of the house. It took Ismael a few seconds to realise what the dull, muffled sounds were. Metal. Something or someone was banging against a piece of metal somewhere in the house. Ismael could feel the vibration beneath his feet and his eyes paused on a closed door in the passage that led to the kitchen.

'Where does that door go?'

'To the cellar,' Irene replied.

Ismael put his ear on the wooden panel and listened carefully. The knocks were repeated again and again. He tried to open the door, but the handle wouldn't turn.

'Is someone in there?' he shouted.

They could hear the sound of footsteps, coming up the stairs.

'Be careful,' whispered Irene.

Ismael moved away from the door. A faint voice could be heard on the other side. Irene hurled herself at the wooden panel.

'Dorian?'

The voice muttered something.

Irene looked at Ismael.

'It's my brother . . .'

Ismael quickly realised that to break down a door was much more difficult than Hollywood films led you to believe. It was a good five minutes before the door finally yielded with the help of a metal bar they found in the larder. Covered in sweat, Ismael moved back and Irene gave the door a final pull. The lock – by now just a tangle of wooden splinters and rusty metal – fell to the floor.

A second later, a pale boy emerged from the darkness, his face rigid with fear. Dorian sheltered in his sister's arms, like a frightened animal. Irene glanced at Ismael. Whatever it was that Dorian had seen, it had left its mark on him. Irene knelt down and cleaned the dirt and tears off his face.

'Are you all right, Dorian?' she asked calmly, feeling his body for wounds or broken bones.

Dorian nodded.

'Where is Mum?'

His eyes filled with anguish.

'Dorian, this is important. Where is she?'

'She . . . she was taken away,' he babbled.

Ismael wondered how long Dorian had been trapped there, in the dark.

'She was taken away . . .' Dorian repeated, as if in a trance.

'Who has taken her, Dorian?' Irene asked. 'Who has taken our mother?'

Dorian smiled in a strange way, as if the question was absurd.

'The shadow,' he replied. 'The shadow took her.'

Irene took a deep breath and put her hands on her brother's shoulders.

'Dorian, I'm going to ask you to do something very important. Do you understand?'

Her brother nodded.

'I want you to get to the village as fast as you can. Go to the police station, and tell the superintendent there's been a terrible accident in Cravenmoore. Tell him Mum is there and she's been hurt. Tell the police to come immediately. Do you understand?'

Dorian looked bewildered.

'Don't mention the shadow. Just tell the superintendent what I said. It's very important . . . If you talk about the shadow, nobody will believe you. You must just say there's been an accident.'

Ismael nodded in agreement.

'I need you to do this for me, and for Mum. Will you do it?'

Dorian looked at Ismael, then at his sister.

'Our mother's had an accident at Cravenmoore. She needs help urgently,' the boy repeated mechanically. 'But she's all right . . . isn't she?'

Irene smiled and hugged him.

'I love you,' she whispered.

Dorian kissed his sister on the cheek and went off in search of his bicycle. He found it leaning against the wooden rail on the porch. Lazarus's gift was now just a mangled heap of cables and twisted metal. Dorian was still staring at the wreckage of his bicycle when Ismael and Irene appeared from the house.

'Who would do something like this?' asked Dorian.

'You'd better hurry,' Irene reminded him.

He set off at a run. As soon as he'd disappeared, Irene and Ismael walked back onto the porch. The sun was setting over the bay, a dark orb bleeding through the clouds. Their eyes met. They knew what awaited them in the heart of darkness, beyond the forest.

12. DOPPELGÄNGER

'There has never been a more beautiful bride standing at the altar,' said the mask. 'Never. I know most men will say that, but few truly believe it. I did and I do.

'The happiness Alexandra brought into my life blotted out all the memories and misery that had filled my childhood. Such is the blessing of true love to those very few who experience it. It makes everything else irrelevant. God is cruel, for most of his creatures go through their empty lives without even being able to imagine what that is. True love also changes who we are. I stopped being that wretched boy from the poorest district of Paris. I forgot the long imprisonments in the dark and consigned the memory of my mother to the past. All of it I left behind me. And do you know why? Because Alexandra Alma Maltisse, my saviour, taught me that, contrary to what my mother had told me over and over again, I was not a bad person. That I deserved to be loved. Do you understand, Simone? I wasn't evil. I was just like everyone else. I was innocent.'

Lazarus paused for a moment. Simone pictured the tears behind the mask.

'Together, we explored Cravenmoore. A lot of

people think that the marvels contained in this house are all my own creation. However only a small selection of them originate from my hands. The rest, all those endless galleries of amazing machines that even I don't understand, were already here when I first moved in. I'll never know how long they were here before I came. There was a time when I thought that others had occupied my place before me. Sometimes, if I stop to listen in the dead of night, I think I can hear the echoes of other voices, other footsteps, filling the corridors. Sometimes I think that perhaps time has stood still in every room, in every empty passageway, and that the creatures who inhabit this mansion were once human beings, just like me.

'I stopped worrying about such matters long ago, however, even though I was still discovering new rooms I'd never been in before after I'd lived in Cravenmoore for years. New corridors that led to wings I'd never seen . . . I think that some places – ancient dwellings that can be counted on the fingers of one hand – are so much more than a building; they're alive. They have their own soul and their own way of communicating with us. Cravenmoore is one of those places. Nobody knows when it was built. Nor who built it, now why. But when this house speaks to me, I listen . . .

'Before that summer of 1916, when we were at our happiest, something happened. In fact, in had begun to happen a year before that, although I didn't realise it. The day after our wedding, Alexandra got up at dawn and went into the large oval hall to look at the hundreds of presents we'd received. The gift that first caught her eye was a small hand-carved casket. A gem. Captivated, Alexandra opened it. It contained a note and a glass bottle. The note, which was addressed to her, said that this was a special gift. A surprise. It explained that the bottle contained my favourite perfume, the one my mother had used, and that she should wait until the day of our first anniversary before using it. This was to remain a secret between her and the person who had signed the note, an old friend from my childhood, Daniel Hoffmann . . .

'Following his instructions to the letter, and convinced that by doing so she would make me happy, Alexandra kept the bottle for twelve months. On the agreed date, she took it out of the casket and opened it. Needless to say the bottle didn't contain perfume. It was the flask I'd thrown into the sea on the eve of our wedding. From the moment Alexandra opened it, our life turned into a nightmare . . .

'Around the same time I began to receive letters from Daniel Hoffmann. He wrote to me from Berlin, where he said he was involved in a great task that would one day change the world. Millions of children were receiving his gifts. Millions of children who would, one day, form the greatest army ever known. I still don't understand what he meant by those words.

'In one of his early parcels, he sent me a book, a leather-bound volume that seemed older than the world itself. There was just one word on the cover:

"Doppelgänger". Have you ever heard of a doppelgänger? Of course you haven't. Nowadays, nobody is interested in legends and magic. Doppelgänger was originally a Germanic term, meaning a shadow that becomes detached from its owner and turns against him. The book was basically a manual about shadows. A museum piece. And by the time I started reading it, it was too late. Something was already lurking in the darkness of this house; growing secretly, month after month, like a snake's egg waiting to hatch.

'By May 1916 the brightness of that first year with Alexandra was beginning to fade. Soon I realised that the shadow had come back. The first attacks were only minor incidents. Alexandra would find her clothes torn to shreds. Doors would slam shut as she approached them and invisible hands would push objects towards her. There were voices in the dark. That was just the beginning . . .

'This house has a thousand dark corners where a shadow can hide. It struck me then that Cravenmoore was in fact the soul of its creator, of Daniel Hoffmann, and that the shadow would grow within that soul, getting stronger day by day, while I became weaker. All the strength I had once possessed would become the property of the shadow and slowly, as I moved back into the darkness of my childhood, I would end up becoming the shadow, and Hoffmann my master.

'I decided to close the toy factory and concentrate on my former obsession: I wanted to bring Gabriel back to life, the guardian angel who had protected me in

Paris. I felt that, if I managed to make the angel come alive, it would protect me and Alexandra from the shadow. That's why I set about designing the most powerful automaton I had ever dreamed of. A steel colossus. An angel that would free me from my nightmare.

'How naïve . . . The moment that monstrous construction was able to rise from the table in my workshop, any hint of obedience disappeared. It wasn't me the angel listened to, but its master, the shadow. And its master could not exist without me, because I was the source of its power. Not only did the angel *not* rid me of my nightmare, it turned into the worst guardian imaginable. The guardian of the terrible secret that condemned me for eternity, a guardian that would rise without pity every time something or someone put that secret at risk.

'The attacks on Alexandra intensified. The shadow was now more powerful and with every day the threat grew stronger. The shadow had decided to punish me through my wife's suffering. I had given Alexandra a heart that did not belong to me and that mistake would be our undoing. I was close to losing my mind when I noticed that the shadow only acted if I was nearby. It couldn't live without me. That is why I decided to abandon Cravenmoore and take refuge in the lighthouse. It wouldn't be able to hurt anyone there, on the island. If someone was to pay the price of my betrayal, that someone had to be me. But I had underestimated Alexandra's strength. Her love for me.

Overcoming her terror and risking her own life, she came to my rescue on the night of the masked ball. As soon as the boat in which she was sailing approached the island, the shadow fell on her and dragged her to the bottom of the sea. I can still hear its laughter when it surfaced through the waves. The following day, it returned to the glass bottle. For the next twenty years I didn't see it again . . .'

Simone stood up, trembling, and slowly retreated until she backed into the wall. She couldn't listen to another word from this man's lips, from this sick person. Only one thing kept her where she was and stopped her from giving in to the panic she felt after hearing the masked figure's story: her anger.

'No, dear friend . . . Don't make that mistake . . . Don't you understand what's happening? When you and your family arrived here, I couldn't help but let my heart notice you. I didn't intend to do so. I didn't even realise what was happening until it was too late. I tried to break the spell by building a machine in your own image . . .'

'What?'

'I thought . . . Shortly after your arrival, which filled this house with life again, the shadow awoke from its limbo. It had been asleep for twenty years in that accursed bottle but it soon found a victim to release it again.'

'Hannah . . .' Simone murmured.

'I know what you must be thinking, but believe me, there is no possible escape. I've done everything I can . .

The masked man stood up and walked towards her.

'Don't take another step!' Simone screamed.

Lazarus stopped.

'I don't want to hurt you, Simone. I'm your friend. Don't turn your back on me.'

She felt a wave of loathing.

'You murdered Hannah . . .'

'Simone . . .'

'Where are my children?'

'They've chosen their fate . . .'

An icy dagger ripped at her heart.

'What have you done with them?'

Lazarus raised his gloved hands.

'They're dead . . .'

Before he could finish his sentence, Simone let out a furious yell and, grabbing one of the candlesticks from the table, she threw herself at the man standing in front of her. The base of the candlestick struck the middle of the mask and the porcelain face shattered into a thousand pieces. Behind it there was nothing.

Paralysed with fear, Simone focused on the black mass floating before her. The form threw off its white gloves, beneath which there was nothing but darkness. Only then did Simone see the demonic face taking shape; it slowly acquired volume, hissing like a furious snake. A shriek pierced her ears, a high-pitched howl that extinguished every flame burning in the room. For the first and last time, Simone heard the real voice of the shadow. Then two claws seized her and dragged her out into the night.

As they stepped out of the forest, Ismael and Irene noticed that the soft mist covering the undergrowth was slowly morphing into a glowing mantle. Ahead, Cravenmoore was completely illuminated, light pouring from every window, making the entire structure look like a ghostly ship rising from the ocean.

They stopped in front of the spear-headed gates that led into the garden. Bathed in the strange luminescence, the house looked even more menacing than it did in the dark. On the breeze they could hear the disturbing sound of dozens of automatons moving about inside the mansion. The fiendish cacophony wafted through the front door, which stood wide open. Through it, they could see the shapes of shadows dancing in time to the blood-curdling melody. Instinctively Irene pressed Ismael's hand.

'You don't have to come with me. After all, she's my mother . . .' offered Irene.

'Tempting. Don't ask me twice,' said Ismael.

Trying not to think too hard about the laughter, the music, and the sinister parade of figures inhabiting the place, they began to climb the main staircase.

'Can you feel it too?' asked Ismael as they stepped across the threshold of the front door.

Irene nodded. 'The house. It is waiting for us.'

Dorian knocked repeatedly on the door of the police station. He was out of breath and his legs felt as if they were going to melt. He'd run like someone possessed through the forest, down to the Englishman's Beach, and then along the endless road that bordered the bay. He hadn't stopped for a second, knowing that if he did he wouldn't be able to take another step. A single thought drove him forward: the image of that terrible shape carrying off his mother into the night. He had only to remember that and he'd run to the end of the world.

When the door of the police station finally opened, the rotund figure of Gendarme Jobart appeared. His tiny eyes examined the boy, who looked as if he was about to collapse.

'Well?' spat out the police officer.

'Water, please . . .'

'This is not a bar, Comrade Sauvelle.'

Shaking his head in disapproval Jobart let the boy in and gave him a glass of water. Dorian had never known that water could be so delicious.

'More.'

Jobart handed him another glassful.

'You're welcome.'

Dorian finished the last drop and then looked up at the policeman. Irene's instructions came to mind, loud and clear.

'My mother has had an accident and she's hurt. It's serious. At Cravenmoore.'

'What sort of accident?'

'We need to go *now*!' Dorian burst out.

'I'm alone. I can't leave my post.'

Dorian suppressed a sigh. Of all the idiots on the face of the planet he'd gone and found a prize one.

'Use the radio! Do *something*!'

The clear anxiety in Dorian's tone finally prompted Jobart to move his considerable backside. He walked over to the radio and switched on the machine. For a moment he turned to look at the boy.

'Go on! Hurry!' Dorian shouted.

Lazarus regained consciousness abruptly and felt a sharp pain in the back of his neck. He lifted a hand and touched the open wound. He vaguely remembered Christian's face looming at him in the corridor of the west wing. The automaton had struck him and dragged him to this place. Lazarus looked around. He was in one of the many disused rooms of Cravenmoore.

Slowly, he stood up and tried to put his thoughts in order. Deep exhaustion washed over him. He closed his eyes and took a deep breath. When he opened them again, he noticed a small mirror hanging on one of the walls. He walked over to it and stared at his reflection. Then he crossed to a tiny window overlooking the main façade. He noticed two figures stealing across the garden towards the front door.

Irene and Ismael stepped into the beam of light coming from deep inside the house. The echo of the merry-go-round and the metallic rattling of thousands of cogs that had been brought to life chilled them to the bone. A whole world of impossible creatures jiggled about in glass cabinets or dangled from the ceiling. It was impossible to look in any direction and not find one of Lazarus's creations in motion. Clocks with faces, dolls that looked as if they were sleepwalking, ghostly faces with teeth bared like hungry wolves . . .

'This time I'd prefer it if we didn't separate,' said Irene.

'Wasn't planning to,' Ismael replied.

They'd only gone a couple of metres when the main door slammed shut behind them. Irene screamed and clung to Ismael. A gigantic man stood before them, his face covered with a mask depicting a ghoulish clown with green eyes. The monster's pupils dilated and it began to walk towards them, a large carving knife in its hand. Suddenly, Irene recalled the mechanical butler that had opened the door on their first visit to Cravenmoore. Christian. That was his name. The figure raised the knife in the air.

'No, Christian!' she shouted. 'No!'

The butler stopped and the knife fell from its hand. Ismael looked at Irene, confused. The motionless automaton was watching them.

'Quick,' Irene insisted, and moved off towards the centre of the house.

Ismael ran after her, but first he picked up the knife Christian had dropped. He caught up with Irene in the stairwell that rose towards the high domed ceiling. Irene looked around and tried to get her bearings.

'Where now?' asked Ismael, looking over his shoulder.

She hesitated, unable to decide which way to go.

Suddenly, they felt a gust of cold air blowing along one of the corridors. With it came the sound of a deep, cavernous voice.

'Irene . . .' the voice intoned.

Irene's stomach tied itself up in knots. The voice came again. She stared at the end of the corridor. Ismael followed the direction of her gaze. And there, floating above the ground, enveloped in a cloud of smoke, was Simone, advancing towards them with outstretched arms. There was a diabolical glow in her eyes and two lines of steely fangs appeared behind her pale lips.

'Mum,' moaned Irene.

'That isn't your mother . . .' said Ismael, drawing the girl away from the creature's path. As the light caught its features, the full horror of the beast was revealed. Only half of its face was finished; the other half was just a metal mask. It turned to confront them once more.

'It's the doll we saw before, not your mother,' Ismael repeated, trying to waken his friend from the trance into which she seemed to have plunged. 'That thing, the shadow, moves them as if they were its puppets . . .'

The mechanism inside the automaton made a clicking sound and it rushed at them, its claws bared. Ismael grabbed Irene and fled, without quite knowing where they were going. They ran as fast as their legs could carry them, through a gallery with doors on either side that opened as they passed.

'Quick!' shouted Ismael, as he heard the shrill of mechanical cables behind him.

Irene turned her head. The wolf-like jaws of the replica of her mother snapped shut only twenty centimetres from her face. Needle-sharp talons reached towards her. Ismael pulled Irene to one side, into what looked like a large dark hall, and closed the door behind them. The creature's claws sank into the door like lethal arrows.

'My God . . .' Irene gasped. 'Not again . . .'

She was as white as a sheet.

'Are you all right?' Ismael asked.

She nodded vaguely and then gazed around her. Walls of books seemed to spiral towards infinity.

'We're in Lazarus's library.'

'Well, I hope there's another way out, because I'm not going back there,' said Ismael.

'There must be another exit. I just don't know where . . .' she said, heading towards the centre of the room.

Ismael wedged the door shut with a chair. If his defences lasted more than two minutes, he thought, he'd start to believe in miracles. Behind him, Irene murmured something. He turned and saw that she was standing next to a table, examining a book. It looked ancient.

'There's something here,' she said.

A dark foreboding took hold of him.

'Put down that book . . .'

'Why?' asked Irene, puzzled.

'Put it down.'

Irene closed the book and did as her friend asked. The gold letters on the cover shone in the light of the blaze from the fireplace: 'Doppelgänger'.

Irene had only just left the desk when she felt a strong vibration under her feet. The fire in the hearth flickered and some of the tomes on the bookshelves began to shake. The girl ran to Ismael.

'What the hell . . .?' said Ismael. The intense rumbling seemed to be coming from the very depths of the house.

At that moment, the book Irene had left on the desk burst open and the flames in the fireplace were extinguished by a blast of icy air. Ismael put his arms around Irene and drew her close. Books started to tumble down from on high, pushed by invisible hands.

'There's someone here,' Irene whispered. 'I can feel it . . .'

The pages of the book slowly began to turn over one by one. Ismael gazed at the ancient volume. He noticed for the first time that the letters on its pages appeared to be evaporating, forming a gaseous black cloud above the book. The shapeless mass was absorbing word after word, sentence after sentence, a phantom of black ink suspended in mid-air.

Suddenly the dark cloud expanded and the shapes of hands, arms and a trunk appeared, together with a sphinx-like face.

Petrified with fear, Ismael and Irene watched as the electrifying apparition, and other shapes around it, came to life from the pages of the fallen books. Slowly, an entire army of shadows formed before their incredulous eyes. Shadows of children, of old men, of women dressed in strange costumes . . . trapped spirits, too weak to acquire consistency and volume. Their anguished faces were weary and listless. As she looked at them, Irene felt she was standing before lost souls, beings enslaved by some terrible curse. They stretched out their hands towards her, begging for help, but their fingers faded, becoming nothing more than a nebulous mass. She could feel the horror of the darkness that gripped them.

Irene wondered who these spirits were and how they'd got there. Had they once been unsuspecting visitors to Cravenmoore, just as she was? For a moment she thought she might spot her mother among them, but at a simple gesture from the shadow, their forms melted into a dark whirlwind that swept across the room.

The shadow opened its jaws and swallowed each and every one of them, consuming what little strength they had left. A deathly silence followed. Then the shadow opened its eyes. They shone blood-red in the gloom.

Irene wanted to scream, but her voice was lost in the sudden roar that shook Cravenmoore. One by one, all the windows and doors of the house were being sealed up, like tombstones closing. Ismael heard a cavernous echo rumble through the corridors of Cravenmoore and sensed that their hopes of getting out of there alive were quickly evaporating.

Now only a thin line of brightness remained, a tightrope of light high up on the vaulted ceiling. Without waiting another second, Ismael grabbed Irene's hand and felt his way towards to the other end of the room.

'Perhaps the other exit is up there,' he whispered.

Irene looked up in the direction Ismael was pointing, at the thread of light which seemed to be coming through a keyhole. The library was constructed in a series of concentric ovals, connected by a narrow passageway that rose in a spiral up the walls and led to the different galleries that branched out from it. Simone had told her about this architectural quirk: if you followed the passageway to the end you were almost level with the third floor of the house. It was a sort of indoor Tower of Babel, Irene thought. This time she led the way.

'Do you know where you're going?' asked Ismael.

'Trust me.'

He hurried after Irene, the ground slowly rising underfoot as they went further into the passageway. A cold draught caressed the back of his neck and he noticed that there was a thick black stain spreading across the floor behind him. The shadow's texture was viscous now, and it moved like a sheet of oil, thick and shiny.

After a few seconds, it reached Ismael's feet. The boy felt a cold spasm, as if he were walking on ice.

'Hurry!' he cried.

As they had suspected, the thread of light was coming from a door, which was now only half a dozen metres away from them. Ismael ran towards it, managing to get ahead of the shadow for a few moments. He doubted the door would be unlocked.

Irene's hands were already on the lock, searching for some way of opening it. Ismael turned to check where the shadow was and discovered the jet-black mantle rising before him. A tar-like face materialised. A familiar face. Ismael thought his eyes were playing tricks on him. He blinked. The face was still there. It was his own.

Ismael's dark reflection gave him an evil smile, a reptilian tongue flickering out of its mouth. Instinctively, Ismael pulled out the knife he'd taken from the butler Christian and brandished it in front of the shadow. The figure blew on the weapon and a sheen of frost spread from the point of the blade to the hilt. The frozen metal sent an intense burning sensation through the palm of his hand. Ismael almost let go of the weapon, but he ignored the spasm gripping his forearm and tried to plunge the knife into the shadow's face. The blade touched the shadow's tongue and dropped off, falling by Ismael's feet. Instantly, the small mass wrapped itself around his ankle like a second skin and then began to creep up his leg. The contact with its slimy matter made him feel nauseous.

Just then, he heard the lock give a click and a tunnel of light opened up before them. Irene ran through the door, followed by Ismael, who slammed it shut, leaving his pursuer on the other side. The knife blade that had become detached had now reached his thigh and it took on the shape of a giant spider. A painful cramp shot up his leg. Irene tried to brush off the monstrous insect but the spider turned towards her and jumped on her. Irene let out a terrified scream.

'Get it off me!'

By now Ismael had discovered the source of the light that had been guiding them. A row of candles extended into the gloom. The boy grabbed one of them and held the flame next to the spider, which was heading towards Irene's throat. The contact with the fire made the creature hiss in anger and pain, then it disintegrated into black droplets that rained down on the floor. Ismael put down the candle and pulled Irene away from the fragments. The drops slithered like jelly over the floor then joined into a single body that slid back under the door.

'Fire! It's afraid of fire,' said Irene.

Ismael picked up the candle and placed it by the door, while Irene took a quick look around. The space had probably once served as an additional storeroom for the library but it seemed more like an empty waiting room, with no furniture and covered in decades of dust. On closer inspection, Irene noticed shapes on the ceiling. Small pipes. Irene took one of the candles and lifted it above her head. She could see the glint of tiles and mosaics on the wall.

'Where the hell are we?' asked Ismael.

'I don't know . . . They look like . . . like showers . .

'

In the candlelight they could see a network of hundreds of bell-shaped sprinklers emerging from the pipes, their mouths rusty and covered in a citadel of cobwebs.

'Whatever this place is, it must be ages since anyone has—'

Before she'd even finished the sentence, they heard a harsh sound, the unmistakable screech of a rusty wheel turning. Right there, next to them. Irene brought the candle closer to the tiled wall. There were two stopcocks, and they were moving.

A strong vibration was running through the walls, the rumble of something creeping above their heads. They held their breath. Something was making its way through the narrow pipes.

'It's here!' shouted Irene.

Ismael nodded, his eyes glued to the sprinklers. A thick mass began to filter through the holes. Irene and Ismael took a few steps back, transfixed as the shadow gradually formed before them, like sand falling through an hourglass.

Two eyes appeared and the friendly face of Lazarus smiled at them. It would have been a reassuring sight had they not known that what was standing before them was not Lazarus.

'Where is my mother?' Irene asked defiantly, moving closer.

A deep, inhuman voice spoke: 'She's with me . . .'

'Get away from him,' said Ismael.

The shadow's eyes locked on Ismael, who appeared to go into a trance. Irene shook her friend and tried to move him away, but he did not react and remained trapped in the shadow's spell. She put herself in between the two then slapped Ismael, which finally woke him from his stupor. The face of the shadow now filled with anger and two long arms reached towards them. Irene and Ismael hurled themselves against the wall, trying to dodge the shadow's claws.

At that moment a door opened and a halo of light appeared on the other side of the room. In the doorway stood a man holding an oil lamp.

'Get out of here!' he yelled. Irene immediately recognised the voice: it was the toymaker, Lazarus Jann.

The shadow let out a shriek, and one by one the candles went out. Lazarus advanced towards the shadow. His face seemed much older than Irene remembered and his bloodshot eyes were immensely tired, like those of a man consumed by illness.

'Get out of here!' he shouted again.

They caught a glimpse of the shadow's demonic face as it transformed into a cloud of gas, seeping into the cracks in the floor and flowing towards a small gap in the wall. As it escaped, it made a sound similar to wind whistling against windowpanes.

Lazarus stood there, watching the gap for a moment. Then he fixed his penetrating gaze on Irene and Ismael.

'What on earth are you doing here?' he asked, unable to hide his fury.

'I've come to find my mother. I'm not leaving without her,' Irene retorted.

'You don't know what you're up against . . . Quick, this way. It won't be long before it comes back.'

Lazarus led them through the door.

'What *is* this thing? What is it we've seen?' asked Ismael.

Lazarus looked at him intently.

'It's me . . . That thing you've seen is me . . .'

Lazarus led them through an intricate labyrinth of tunnels, the very bowels of Cravenmoore. The way was flanked by a large number of closed doors on either side, secret entrances to the dozens of bedrooms and other rooms in the house..

Lazarus's lamp cast a circle of amber light against the walls. Ismael noticed his own shadow and Irene's walking beside them, but Lazarus had no shadow. The toymaker stopped before a tall narrow door, pulled out a key, then opened it. He scanned the passage along which they had come and signalled to them to go in.

'This way,' he said nervously. 'It won't come back here, at least for a few minutes . . .'

Ismael and Irene were suspicious.

'You have no option but to trust me,' Lazarus warned them.

Ismael sighed and stepped inside the room with Irene and Lazarus following. The lamplight revealed a wall covered with photographs and cuttings. At one end stood a small bed and an empty desk. Lazarus put the lamp on the floor and watched as the two young people examined the bits of paper.

'You *must* leave Cravenmoore while there's still time.'

Irene turned to him.

'You're not the ones it wants,' added the toymaker. 'It's after your mother, Simone.'

'Why? What does it want to do to her?'

Lazarus looked down.

'It wants to destroy her. In order to punish me. And it will do the same to you if you get in its way. You must leave this place. Sooner or later it will return, and this time I won't be able to protect you.'

At that moment a distant boom was heard somewhere in the house. Irene gulped and looked at Ismael. Footsteps. One after the other, exploding like gunshots, and getting closer and closer. Lazarus smiled faintly.

'Here it comes,' he announced. 'You don't have much time left.'

'Where is my mother? Where have you taken her?' Irene demanded.

'I don't know, but even if I did, it wouldn't be any use.'

'You built that machine with her face . . .' Ismael said.

'I thought it would be satisfied with that, but it wanted more. It wanted her.'

By now the demonic footsteps were approaching their refuge.

211

'On the other side of that door, over there,' Lazarus explained, 'there's a gallery leading to the main staircase. If you have a drop of common sense, you'll run away and leave this house for ever.'

'We're not going anywhere,' said Ismael firmly. 'Not without Irene's mother.'

The door through which they had entered shook powerfully. A second later, a black stain spread beneath the doorway.

'Let's get out of here,' Ismael urged Irene.

The shadow wrapped itself around the lamp and the glass cracked. Then the flame went out. In the gloom, Lazarus watched as Irene and Ismael fled through the other exit. Next to him towered a figure, black and impenetrable.

'Leave them alone,' he groaned. 'They're only children. Let them go. Take me once and for all, isn't that what you want?'

The shadow smiled.

The gallery in which they found themselves crossed the central point of Cravenmoore. Irene recognised the place where the corridors all met and led Ismael to the spot beneath the dome. Clouds could be seen through the glass windows of the turret, scudding across the night sky.

'This way,' said Irene.

'This way, where?' asked Ismael nervously.

'I think I know where it's taken her.'

Ismael turned to look behind them. There was no

sign of movement in the darkness, although he realised that the shadow could easily advance towards them without them being aware of it.

'I hope you know what you're doing,' he replied.

'Follow me.'

Irene headed off down one of the wings and Ismael followed. Slowly, the light from the dome faded and they became aware of the swaying silhouettes of the mechanical creatures populating both sides of the corridor. Voices, laughter and the whirring of metal parts drowned out the sound of their steps. Ismael looked behind them once more, scanning the entrance to the tunnel as a gust of cold air blew towards them. Looking ahead, Ismael recognised the gauzy curtains fluttering in front of him, marked with the initial A.

'I'm sure this is where he's keeping her,' said Irene.

Beyond the curtains, at the end of the corridor, stood the carved wooden door. It was closed.

A new breath of air enveloped them, stirring the gauzy veils.

Tense as a steel cable, Ismael froze, trying to discern something in the gloom.

'What's the matter?' asked Irene, sensing his apprehension.

He opened his mouth to reply but then stopped. Irene looked down the corridor behind them. There was a point of light at the end, but the rest was darkness.

'It's there,' said Ismael. 'Watching us.'

Irene drew close to him.

'Can't you feel it?'

'Let's not stay here, Ismael.'

He nodded, but his thoughts were elsewhere. Irene took his hand and led him to the door at the end. Without saying a word, Ismael placed his hand on the knob and turned it slowly. The door yielded with a faint metal click and swung open on its hinges.   Irene advanced a few steps. An eerie blue mist filled the room. Everything was as she remembered it. The large portrait of Alma Maltisse presided over the fireplace and the fine silk curtains billowed gently around the four-poster bed. Ismael carefully closed the door and followed Irene, but then she stopped him. She pointed to an armchair facing the fireplace. They could see only the back of it, but from one of its arms hung a pale hand, drooping onto the floor.

Next to the hand shiny fragments of broken wineglass lay scattered in a pool of liquid. Irene let go of Ismael's hand and crept towards the armchair. In the flickering light of the fire she could see a drowsy face: her mother.

Irene knelt down next to her and took her hand. For a few seconds she couldn't find a pulse.

'Oh God . . .'

Ismael rushed over to the desk and picked up a small silver tray. He ran to Simone and placed the tray in front of her face. A faint hint of breath clouded the surface. Irene took a deep breath.

'She's alive,' said Ismael, gazing at the unconscious face of the woman. She looked to him like a mature version of Irene.

'We have to get her out of here. Help me.'

They stood on either side of Simone and, putting their arms around her, tried to lift her from the armchair.

They'd only managed to raise her a few centimetres when they heard a deep, chilling whisper from somewhere inside the room.

'Let's not waste any time,' Irene urged.

Ismael attempted to lift Simone again, but this time the sound was much closer and he realised where it was coming from. The portrait. In an instant, the thin film covering the oil painting bulged out, forming a sheet of liquid darkness. As it gained substance it unfolded two long arms ending in claws as sharp as daggers.

Ismael tried to move back, but the shadow jumped from the wall like a cat, leaping through the air and landing behind him. For a second, the only thing Ismael could see was his own shadow watching him. Then another form emerged from the shape, spreading over it until it had swallowed it completely. The boy could feel Simone's body slipping from his arms. A powerful icy claw wrapped itself round his neck then hurled him against the wall.

'Ismael!' shouted Irene.

The shadow turned towards her. She ran to the other end of the room, but the blackness at her feet closed about her, taking on the form of a deadly flower. She felt the chilling contact as it enveloped her body and numbed her muscles. Struggling hopelessly, she stared in horror as the dark mantle dropped from the ceiling and morphed into a familiar face – Hannah's. The ghostly mask threw her a look full of hatred and its lips opened to reveal long fangs, wet and shining.

'You're not Hannah,' said Irene, her voice tiny.

The shadow struck her, gashing her cheek. Instantly, the drops of blood from the wound were absorbed by it, as if it were drinking them in. Irene felt a wave of nausea. Brandishing two long, pointed fingers in front of her eyes, the shadow drew closer still.

As Ismael was getting back on his feet, still dazed by the blow, he saw that the shadow was holding Irene captive in the middle of the room and was about to kill her. Ismael yelled and threw himself against the black mass. His body went straight through it and the shadow split into thousands of tiny droplets that fell to the floor like liquid coal. Ismael lifted Irene and pulled her away from the shadow's reach. On the floor, the pieces came together, forming a whirlwind that hurled the furniture towards the walls and windows.

Ismael and Irene flung themselves to the ground as the desk crashed through one of the windowpanes, shattering it completely. Ismael rolled over Irene, protecting her from the impact. When he looked up again, the whirlwind was solidifying. Two great black wings unfolded and the shadow emerged, larger and more powerful than before.

Ismael pulled out his knife again and wielded it in front of the shadow. The spectre grasped the blade with its icy claw. Ismael could feel the freezing current rising up his fingers and through his hand, paralyzing his arm.

The weapon fell and the shadow wrapped itself around the boy. Irene tried in vain to pull him away. The shadow started dragging Ismael towards the fire.

At that very moment the door burst open, and Lazarus appeared on the threshold.

The ghostly light emerging from the forest reflected off the windscreen of the police car at the head of the convoy. Behind it were Doctor Giraud's vehicle and an ambulance sent by the clinic at La Rochelle.

Dorian, sitting next to the superintendent, Henri Faure, was the first to notice the golden glow filtering through the trees. The top of Cravenmoore could be glimpsed above the forest. It looked like an apparition, a gigantic merry-go-round, in the mist. The superintendent frowned – he'd never seen such a sight in the fifty-two years he'd been living in the village.

'Faster!' Dorian urged him.

As he accelerated, the superintendent glanced at the boy, wondering whether the story of the supposed accident contained a single grain of truth.

'Is there something you haven't told us?'

Dorian didn't reply but kept staring straight ahead.

The superintendent pressed the accelerator to the floor.

The shadow whirled round and, when it saw Lazarus, it dropped Ismael suddenly. The boy hit the ground hard and screamed out in pain. Irene ran to his aid.

'Get him out of here,' said Lazarus, as he advanced towards the shadow, which was retreating.

Ismael groaned. There was a sharp pain in his shoulder.

'Are you all right?' asked Irene.

Ismael mumbled something, but then he got to his feet and nodded. Lazarus gave them an inscrutable look.

'Take your mother and leave,' he said.

The shadow was hissing in front of him like a snake ready to strike. Suddenly it jumped onto the wall and melted into the painting once more.

'I said go!' Lazarus shouted.

Ismael and Irene grabbed hold of Simone and hauled her towards the door. As they were about to leave, Irene turned to look at Lazarus. She watched as the toymaker walked over to the four-poster bed and, with infinite tenderness, drew aside the veils that covered it. The figure of a woman could be seen through the curtains.

'Wait . . .' whispered Irene, her heart in her mouth.

The woman *had* to be Alma. Irene trembled as she noticed the tears on Lazarus's face. The toymaker hugged his wife. Never in her life had Irene seen anyone hug another person so tenderly. Every gesture, every movement conveyed a love and a tenderness that could only result from a life of complete devotion. Alma's arms closed around him too and, for a magical moment, they were united in the darkness, far from this world. Without knowing why, Irene felt like crying, but then a new vision, terrible and menacing, startled her from her reverie.

The stain was sliding, sinuously, from the portrait towards the bed. Irene felt a wave of panic.

'Lazarus, be careful!'

The toymaker turned and watched as the shadow rose in front of him with a furious roar. For a second, he held the infernal creature's gaze. Then he turned to Irene and Ismael; he seemed to be trying to say something with his eyes, but they couldn't quite understand. Suddenly, Irene realised what Lazarus was about to do.

'No!' she shouted, but Ismael held her back.

The toymaker approached the shadow.

'You won't take her away again . . .'

The shadow raised a claw, ready to attack its owner. Lazarus put his hand in his jacket pocket and pulled out a shiny object. A revolver. The shadow's laughter echoed through the room.

Lazarus pulled the trigger. Ismael stared in bewilderment. Then the toymaker gave a weak smile and the revolver fell from his hands. A dark stain was spreading over his chest. Blood.

The shadow's cry shook the entire mansion. It was a cry of terror.

'No, no . . .' Irene wailed.

Ismael ran over to help the toymaker, but Lazarus raised a hand.

'No. Leave me here with her. And get out of this place,' he whispered, a trickle of blood running from the corner of his mouth.

Ismael took Lazarus in his arms and moved him closer to the bed. As he did so, he was struck by the heart-rending sight of a sad, pale face. Ismael was gazing at Alma Maltisse. Her tearful eyes stared straight back at him, lost in a slumber from which she would never awake.

She was a machine.

All these years, Lazarus had lived with an automaton he had created to preserve the memory of his wife, the memory that the shadow had taken from him.

Thunderstruck, Ismael took a step back. Lazarus looked at him with pleading eyes.

'Leave me alone with her . . . please.'

'But . . . it's only . . .' Ismael began.

'She's all I've got.'

Ismael then realised why the body of the woman who had drowned off the island had never been found. Lazarus had pulled her out of the sea and brought her back to life – not a real existence, but life as a machine. Unable to face the loneliness and the loss of his wife, he'd created a phantom using her body, a sad reflection with which he had lived for twenty years. As he looked into Lazarus's dying eyes, Ismael also knew that, somehow, in the toymaker's heart, Alexandra Alma Maltisse was still alive.

The toymaker gave him one last look, full of pain. The boy nodded his head slowly and returned to Irene's side.

'What . . .?'

'Let's get out of here. Quick,' Ismael urged her.

'But . . .'

'I said let's get out of here!'

Together, they dragged Simone into the corridor. The door slammed shut behind them, sealing Lazarus inside the room. Irene and Ismael then hurried down the corridor as fast as they could, heading for the main staircase and trying to ignore the unearthly howls coming from the other side of the door.

Staggering to his feet, Lazarus Jann confronted the shadow. The spectre threw him a desperate look. The tiny hole made by the bullet was getting larger, and consuming the shadow second by second. Trying to hide, it leaped towards the portrait again, but this time Lazarus took a blazing log and set fire to the painting.

The fire spread over the canvas like waves on a pond. The shadow howled. In the darkness of the library, the pages of the black book also began to smoulder until they too went up in flames.

Lazarus crawled back towards the bed, but the shadow pursued him now, devoured by the flames and leaving a trail of fire behind it. The curtains of the four-poster bed caught fire and the flames spread over the ceiling and the floor, angrily consuming everything in their path. In a matter of seconds the room became an inferno.

The flames burst through one of the windows, scorching the few remaining bits of glass and sucking in the night air. The door of the room collapsed blazing into the corridor. Then, slowly but inexorably, the fire took possession of the entire house.

Walking through the flames, Lazarus pulled out the glass bottle that had held the shadow for so many years, and raised it in his hands. With a cry of despair, the shadow entered the bottle. A spider-web of frost spread across its glass sides. Then Lazarus sealed the bottle and, gazing at it one last time, he cast it into the fire. The flask burst into a thousand pieces; like the dying breath of a curse, the shadow was extinguished for ever. And with it, the toymaker felt his own life slowly slipping away.

When Irene and Ismael emerged through the front door, carrying the unconscious Simone, the flames were already blazing through the second-floor windows. In just a few seconds, the windowpanes burst, one after another, ejecting a storm of molten glass over the garden. They hurried to the entrance of the wood and only when they reached the shelter of the trees did they stop to look back.

Cravenmoore was burning.

13. SEPTEMBER LIGHTS

One by one, the wonderful creatures that had populated Lazarus Jann's universe were destroyed by the flames that night in 1937. Speaking clocks saw their hands melt into red-hot filaments. Ballerinas and orchestras, magicians, witches and chess players, wonders that would never again see the light of day . . . there was no mercy for any of them. Floor by floor, room by room, all the contents of that magical and terrible place were destroyed, leaving only a trail of ashes behind.

Somewhere in that inferno, the photographs and cuttings Lazarus Jann had treasured were consumed. And as the police cars arrived at the ghostly pyre that lit up the sky like dawn at midnight, the eyes of the small tormented boy were sealed for ever.

As long as he lived, Ismael would never forget the final moments of Lazarus and his companion. The last thing he'd glimpsed was Lazarus kissing his wife on the forehead, and he swore to himself that he would keep this secret to the end of his days.

The break of dawn revealed a cloud of ash rolling towards the horizon over the bay. And as the day chased away the sea mist from the Englishman's Beach, the ruins of Cravenmoore emerged above the treetops. Columns of black smoke rose skywards, forming velvet-black trails that reached towards the clouds.

Gradually, the haze concealing the lighthouse island broke up into wings of mist that fluttered away in the early-morning breeze.

Sitting on a blanket of white sand, Irene and Ismael witnessed the last minutes of that long summer's night in 1937. Without a word, they joined hands and watched as the first rays of sun broke through the clouds. The lighthouse rose before them, dark and solitary. A faint smile appeared on Irene's lips as she realised that, somehow, the lights the villagers had seen glowing through the mist would now be extinguished for ever.

'They are at peace now,' she whispered.

Ismael embraced her. 'Let's go home,' he said.

Together they retraced their steps along the shore, heading towards Seaview. And as they walked, a single thought occupied Irene's mind. In a world of lights and shadows, every person, every one of us, needs to find their own way.

Days later, when Irene's mother disclosed what the shadow had told her – the real story of Lazarus Jann and Alma Maltisse – the pieces of the jigsaw puzzle began to fit together. And yet, being able to shed light on what had really happened could not have changed the course of events. A curse had pursued Lazarus Jann, from his tragic childhood to his death. A death that he himself, in his final moments, had realised was his only way out.

Paris, 26 May 1947

Dear Ismael,

I haven't written to you in a very long time. Too long, I'm afraid. But finally, only about a week ago, a miracle occurred. All the letters you've been sending over the years to my old address reached me, thanks to the kindness of a neighbour, an old woman who is almost ninety but has the sharpest memory of anybody I've ever met. She'd kept them all this time, hoping that one day someone would come by and collect them.

Since then I've been reading and rereading your letters, over and over again. They are my most treasured possession. The reasons for my silence, and for this long absence, are difficult for me to explain. Especially to you, Ismael.

Little did those two young people on the beach imagine that on the morning Lazarus Jann's shadow disappeared for ever, a far more terrible shadow was looming over the world. The shadow of war.

When I lost touch with you during these terrible years, I sent you hundreds of letters that never reached you. I still wonder where they are, where all those words, the many things I had to tell you, ended up. I want you to know that, during those dark times, the memory of you, and of that summer in Blue Bay, was what kept me alive, what gave me the strength to survive another day.

226

Dorian enlisted and served for two years in North Africa. He returned with a pile of useless medals and a wound that will leave him with a limp for the rest of his life. He was one of the lucky ones. He came back. You'll be pleased to hear that he finally managed to get a job in the cartography department of the merchant navy and that, whenever his girlfriend Michelle allows him a free moment (you should see her . . .) he travels the world with his compass.

What can I tell you about my mother? I envy her strength and the composure that got us through so many difficult situations. The war years were tough on her, perhaps more so than for us. She never talks about it, but sometimes, when I see her standing quietly by the window, watching people go by, I wonder what is going through her mind. These days, she doesn't leave the house much and spends hours with only a book for company. It's as if she's crossed a bridge and I don't know how to get to the other side . . . Sometimes I catch her looking at old photographs of Dad and hiding her tears.

As for me, I'm well. A month ago I left Saint Bernard's Hospital, where I've been working all these years. It's going to be demolished. I hope the memories of all the suffering and horror I witnessed during the war will vanish along with the building. I don't think I'm the same person either, Ismael. Something has happened inside me.

I witnessed a great many things I'd never imagined could happen . . . There are shadows in this world,

227

Ismael. Shadows far worse than the one against which you and I fought that night in Cravenmoore. Shadows next to which Daniel Hoffmann is almost child's play. Shadows that exist inside each one of us.

Sometimes I'm pleased that my father isn't here to see all this. But you must be thinking I've become someone who lives solely in the past. Not at all. As soon as I read your last letter, my heart skipped a beat. It was as if the sun had come out after ten long years of rain. I returned to the Englishman's Beach, to the island, and once again I sailed across the bay on board the Kyaneos. *I'll always remember those days as the happiest of my life.*

I have to confess a secret. Often, during the winter nights of the war, while shots and screams echoed through the dark, I would let my thoughts wander back there again, to your side, to the day we spent on the lighthouse island. I wish we had never left that place. I wish that day had never ended.

I suppose you'll wonder whether I ever married. The answer is no. Not for lack of suitors, I might add! Modesty aside, I'm still quite successful in that respect. There have been a few boyfriends, here and there. The war years were too difficult to spend them alone, and I'm not as strong as my mother. But that was it. I've learnt that solitude is sometimes a path that leads to peace. And for months that's the only thing I've wanted, peace.

And that is all. Or nothing. How can I begin to explain the feelings, the memories of these past few years? I'd rather wipe them out with a single stroke of the pen. I'd like my most recent memory to be that dawn on the beach and discover that all the rest has just been a bad dream. I'd like to be fifteen again, and not understand the world around me, but that's impossible.

I don't want to go on writing. I want us to speak face to face.

In a week's time, my mother is going off to spend a couple of months with her sister in Aix-en-Provence. That same day, I'll return to the Gare du Nord station and will take a train to Normandy, just as I did ten years ago. I know you'll be waiting for me and that I'll recognise you among the crowd, as I would even if a thousand years had passed. I've known that for a long time now.

An eternity ago, during the worst days of the war, I had a dream. In the dream I was walking along the Englishman's Beach with you. The sun was setting and the island was just visible through the haze. Everything was as it had been: Seaview, the bay . . . Even the ruins of Cravenmoore peeping over the forest. Everything except us. We were an elderly couple. You could no longer go out sailing and my hair was as white as ash. But we were together.

Ever since that dream I've known that one day, no matter when, our moment would come. That in some distant place the September lights would shine again for us and this time there would be no more shadows crossing our path.

This time it would be for ever.